Highlander Unconquered

by

Cynthia Breeding

Ghosts of Culloden, Book 3

Highlander Unconquered

Cover Art by *The Wild Rose Press, Inc.*

The Wild Rose Press, Inc.
PO Box 708
Adams Basin, NY 14410-0708
Visit us at www.thewildrosepress.com

Publishing History
First Edition, 2024
Trade Paperback ISBN 978-1-5092-5720-1
Digital ISBN 978-1-5092-5721-8

Ghosts of Culloden, Book 3
Published in the United States of America

Foreword

The Scottish New Year's Eve festival of "Hogmanay" has its roots in ancient Celtic and Norse lore. Sturdy sticks (hogmanaies) up to ten feet in length were wrapped in animal hide, ignited, and paraded around the town square at midnight. The smoke was believed to ward off evil for the coming year. The torches were then thrown into a river and the townspeople would gather in a large circle dance, which often ended in embracing couples hieing to the nearest place of privacy.

Another tradition was that of "first-footing" which meant the first person to set foot in another person's home after midnight with a gift—mostly whisky— would bring good luck to the inhabitants. Highland hospitality always welcomed strangers and, in the case of first-footing, preferably dark-haired men (who were the antidote to the blond, marauding Viking invaders of auld) would be the first-footers and thus offer protection to the family within.

And so the legend of dark-haired male strangers begins…

Prologue

New Year's Eve, Present Day
Inverness, Scotland

"I think there's one!" Athena—Thea—Ross pointed toward the edge of the crowd of Hogmanay revelers filling Castle Road and scattered over the banks of the River Ness.

Her childhood friends Charlotte and Vi both squinted in the general direction. "One what?" Charlotte asked.

"A Ross tartan. I see several people wearing it."

Vi gave her a skeptical look. "How in the world can you determine that when it's dark and nearly midnight?"

"The torches the men are carrying shed enough light."

"Hmmph. Are you using one of your preternatural powers to see in the dark?"

"Of course not." Not that she had preternatural powers. As a child growing up in Texas, she'd always had an affinity to relate to nature which had made her more aware of…things…that sometimes others didn't notice. That was all.

"Maybe it's your eyes…such an unusual silvery blue color that might have uncanny abilities?" Charlotte gave her a conspiratorial smile. "Now that I think of it, I could maybe write a paranormal story about you.

Something futuristic, maybe, like silver-eyed women warriors."

Thea laughed. Charlotte was a romance writer always coming up with something fanciful. "I wouldn't make much of a warrior, given my predilection toward anti-violence. Besides, I prefer to stick my nose into the past."

"I'll agree with you on that," Vi said. "History can provide great lessons."

"True. It's why we're all here in Scotland, isn't it?" Thea asked. "You want to do an impressive paper for your university on eighteenth-century weaponry used on the Culloden battlefield. Charlotte wants to find a Highlander hero for her next book, and I want to research ancestry, especially the Stuart kings." She moved a few steps in the direction of the group she'd pointed to earlier. "Those could be my relatives."

Charlotte moved closer to peer into the milling group as well. "I don't see them."

"They've blended in with the crowd following that lady with the beautiful auburn hair," Thea replied. "I think they're getting ready to dance."

"We should join them." Charlotte glanced back to where Vi was and then gaped.

Thea turned to look at what had made Charlotte's mouth fall open and then felt her own chin drop too. "Oh, my." Standing beside Vi was a man who looked like a medieval hero who could have graced one of Charlotte's book covers.

"Oh, my, indeed." Charlotte whispered. "I hope Vi doesn't run him off with some caustic remark."

"They seem to be in pretty animated conversation," Thea said.

"Yeah. Like I said…" Charlotte's voice trailed off as Vi waved them away. "I guess that answers that question. Let's go join the dance."

They started down the slope they'd been standing on when Thea noticed something in her peripheral vision. It moved in the shadows and, as she narrowed her eyes and focused, emerged as a man. Like most of the men tonight, he was dressed in a traditional kilt, although she couldn't discern the colors since he stayed semi-concealed in the darkness. Strange that he wasn't actively taking a part in the festivities, though.

As she watched, she saw him suddenly lurch and stumble and then fall.

"There's a man hurt over there. I'm going to see if he's all right."

"He's probably drunk," Charlotte said. "There's been a lot of whisky flowing tonight, in case you haven't noticed."

"Maybe. I just want to make sure he's okay. You go on ahead."

Charlotte hesitated a moment, then shook her head. "Just hurry up," she said as she turned away.

Lifting the heavy skirt of her costume to walk more quickly, Thea approached the man, who was not moving. Now that she was closer, she could see he was a lot larger than she'd thought. The kilt—a Stuart tartan, she could see now—had slipped up, revealing muscular thighs. Maybe he rode horses a lot? His shoulders were wide, too, and his dark hair was long enough to touch his shoulders.

She could not detect any scent of alcohol as she knelt beside him. He was breathing normally, but his eyes were closed. Gently, she touched his arm, feeling the corded strength beneath the fabric of his sleeve. "Sir?"

The man's eyes sprang open. Golden eyes the color of a wolf's and just as piercing. She leaned back, but his hand clasped hers, his gaze never leaving her face.

And she felt herself falling forward into nothingness.

Chapter One

New Year's Eve, 1745
Inverness, Scotland

"Mmmm." His arms wrapped around Thea, pulling her close while his hands roved over her back, pressing her soft breasts against his hard chest. Strong hands that soothed even though the movement brought friction to her nipples and made them tingle for even closer contact.

"Mmmm," she murmured again as his lips brushed hers, teasingly at first, then with more demand. Alan, her husband, was certainly feeling his oats tonight. He was usually so gentle—tentative, even—and this kiss was gaining way more momentum than it usually did. Not that she minded. She was finding the slight roughness of his mouth quite titillating. And…what was he doing now? Applying enough pressure to slowly part her lips and slip his tongue inside. Alan never did that! What had come over him tonight? Perhaps she shouldn't delve into it, but just enjoy the pleasant sensation of what he was doing with his hands and mouth. With a contented sigh, she threaded her hands into his long hair.

Long hair. Alan had short hair. And Alan had been dead for three years.

Thea's eyes sprang open as she pushed against massive shoulders and stared into eyes that glittered like gold in the moonlight. Good lord! She was sprawled on top of the man she had knelt to help.

"Let me go at once!"

His hands fell away instantly, but he made no other move, only kept his gaze trained on her.

"Really, sir. You need to let me go."

An eyebrow lifted. "Ye are the one lying atop me, lass."

"I am not lying…" Her voice trailed off. She was, in fact, lying "atop" him as he said. She could feel the hard ridge of him against a very sensitive part of her and his legs were between hers. Merciful heavens! She was straddling the man.

In her haste to scramble backwards off him, she tangled her legs—and his—in the heavy, long folds of her skirt and flopped across his belly, her face dangerously close to his groin.

Strong hands lifted her, rolling her onto her back. The man loomed over her, propped on his elbows, a corner of his mouth lifting in a half-grin.

"I'd nae deny ye pleasuring me, lassie, but I doona think that was your intent."

For a moment, she just stared at him before her muddled mind understood what he was talking about. And where her mouth was. She narrowed her own eyes. "What kind of a woman do you think I am?"

He sat back, putting distance between them. "I doona ken. Mayhap ye could explain."

Thea pushed herself to a sitting position, gathering her skirts around her, making quite a fuss about it while she tried to gather her thoughts. What in the world had she just been doing? She hadn't kissed a man since Alan died. Hadn't, actually, kissed any man besides Alan. She and Alan had known each other since middle school, been high school sweethearts careful not ever to go "too far" and had married shortly after graduating. She certainly didn't go about seeking strange men out. She knew a lot of women her age did what they called "hooking up," but she wasn't one of them. It was a good thing it was dark because her face was probably beet red.

"I only meant to check on you when you fell, sir. I'm not quite sure why you decided to take advantage of me, but—"

"Take advantage of ye?" That half-grin appeared again. "I would say it was the other way around, lass. Ye landed atop me." The grin widened. "Nae that I minded."

She frowned. "I would never… I am not that kind of woman!"

He sobered and shrugged. "I would nae judge ye." Tilting his head to one side, he studied her. "Ye do kiss rather well."

"Thank…" Thea stopped. What in the world was she doing? Was she really going to thank him for a remark that was…was… Well, she wasn't sure what it was, but this conversation needed to end. She scrambled to her feet.

"I really need to find my friends."

He rose as well. "I'll escort ye. Where will they be?"

She looked around, but no one was in sight. The bank near the river was deserted. Only moonlight played across the narrow cobbled road along its edge, the rest of the area dark. Squinting, she could not see the Best Western across the water nor the cathedral and other buildings. Slowly, her blood started to chill as she realized that something had drastically shifted. For a fleeting moment, she wondered if the devil had loosed warlocks on Hogmanay. It was a time of revelry, after all. The stranger—who could easily have stepped off one of Charlotte's book covers—had tempted her. Hadn't he? Why else would she have been lying on top of him? And kissing him? She gave herself an inward shake. Witches and warlocks didn't exist. She was probably thinking that because of the first-footing myth about dark-haired strangers. It didn't help that this one had wolf-colored eyes, too. Forcing herself to remain calm—Charlotte and Vi always said she was the logical one—she turned to the man.

"Could you explain to me what is going on?"

"Going on?"

"Happening. Where is everyone?"

"Gone home, most likely. 'Tis getting late." He glanced around. "Where were ye to meet your friends?"

"We're staying at the Best Western."

He looked befuddled. "Where?"

"The hotel. Across the river." She pointed to nothingness and knitted her brows. "How are you making it look like the building has disappeared?"

His look turned to one of wariness. "Which buildings have disappeared?"

"The hotel. The cathedral." She waved a hand. "The other stores. And the streetlights. Why aren't they lit?"

He frowned. "'Tis Inverness, lass. Did ye have a wee bit too much whisky? Are ye confusing the town with Edinburgh?"

"No. I am not confusing the city. My friends and I are from Texas—"

"From where?"

"Texas." At his blank look, she added, "In the United States." Good grief! Everyone knew where Texas was.

"Where?" he asked again.

She studied him. Had he completely failed a world geography course? Or maybe he'd just been a lazy student. After all, a man put together so perfectly physically probably didn't think he needed to be overly smart. "You really don't know where Texas is?"

He shook his head. "I've nae heard of it."

He seemed totally serious. She felt a bit sorry for him at that moment and gentled her voice. "It's in America."

"Ah. The English Colonies, then?"

She kept her expression neutral, trying not to laugh at the archaic label. "Well, yes, I guess you could say that, although we declared independence from Britain back in 1776."

Wariness returned to his wolf-like eyes and they darkened. "1776? 'Tis impossible."

She tried not to let herself get abstracted by the change in his eye color from whisky to brandy. He hadn't heard of the Revolution either? "Why do you say that?"

He gave her a steady look. "Because, lass, we have just entered the year 1746."

"1746?" She looked around again, seeing nothing of civilization as she'd known it. She felt her blood chill again. "That's impossible," she whispered.

"It is?" He'd lowered his voice to a soft pitch, as though she might be a skittish horse. "Why?"

He wasn't going to like the answer. Neither was she. There had to be a logical answer. There had to be. She took a deep breath.

"Because it's the twenty-first century."

****

Ian stared at the lass, not sure he'd heard right. Or

perhaps he'd hit his head harder than he thought, when he tripped and fell, and she wasn't real at all. With her strangely-colored eyes that gleamed nearly silver in the moonlight and her long, pale hair she looked more like one of the Fae than human. Not that he'd actually seen a faerie, but Scots, like the Irish, felt it safer not to deny their possible existence.

But her weight atop him had been real. He definitely remembered that feeling when he'd opened his eyes. Her kisses had been passionate, too… He frowned. Why had the lass been so willing one minute and the next acting like he had taken advantage of her?

And why had she mistaken Inverness for a city with large buildings and street lamps? Was it possible she'd escaped from a madhouse in Edinburgh and was confusing her location?

"Do ye have a name, lass?" Perhaps once he knew that, he'd have a better idea of where she was really from. She gave him an annoyed look.

"Of course I have a name," she said. "It's Athena."

He almost groaned. The lass thought she was a Greek goddess. Not that the comparison wasn't accurate. She had a small, straight nose, high cheekbones, and a full mouth that, just minutes ago, he'd been devouring. Her figure aligned with that of a goddess as well, with lush breasts, a small waist and long legs. He remembered those too, since they'd been straddling him in a very encouraging way. At least they had until she'd practically bolted off him. But Greek goddesses didn't wander around the Scottish countryside in the middle of the night. Perhaps she was a bit touched in the head after all.

"Ye think ye are a goddess?" he asked, careful to

keep his voice neutral.

She scowled at him. "Of course not. My mother loved Greek history. I go by Thea. Thea Ross." Then she raised an eyebrow. "I assume you have a name as well?"

"Ian Stuart," he replied absently, thinking about her last name. Ross. That posed another dilemma. Alexander Ross, chief of Pitcalnie, was the nephew of Duncan Forbes, Lord Culloden, who was the lord president of King George's Court-of-Sessions and garrisoned Inverness against the Jacobites. On the other hand, two of the chief's sons, Malcolm and John, were rebel Jacobites. Ian took a deep breath. He might as well find out where the lady stood.

"Do ye favor the English then, or the Jacobites?"

Her scowl deepened. "Neither. I am American. As I've already explained," she added, as though he might be daft.

"Ye have nae explained anything." He frowned back at her. "Ye canna expect me to believe ye are from another century."

"I know it's hard to accept." She sighed. "It's the truth, though."

"'Tis impossible."

"I would agree, except that it happened to me." She paused. "I...I don't know how it happened, but it did."

She looked at him and he saw both fear and uncertainty in her eyes. He smoothed his expression and gentled his voice. "Can ye tell me what ye do ken?"

She drew a shaky breath and nodded. "I was with my friends Charlotte and Vi watching the Hogmanay procession. We were about to join the dance when I saw you stumble. I wasn't sure if you were hurt, so I went over to check. I...knelt beside you and...touched your shoulder. Then…you grabbed me—"

"I grabbed ye?" He shook his head. "I doona remember that."

"Well, you did." She gave him a defiant look. "The last thing I remember was feeling like I was falling into a big void."

He studied her, not knowing what to say. The lass sounded sane enough, but her story didn't make sense. He had been at the Hogmanay festivities—in his century—and he remembered the dance she mentioned. He'd been about to join it when he'd tripped over a root and fallen. But that was all he remembered. He certainly didn't recall the lass kneeling by him or his grabbing her. He wasn't the sort to grab a woman anyway. He'd never needed to, since they came willingly into his arms. Just like Athena had. Until something had frightened her literally off him. He shook his head to clear it. Better to escort the lass to her lodgings and forget the whole matter.

"I ken ye believe what ye're saying, but mayhap ye had a wee bit too much whisky—"

"I am not drunk. I wasn't drunk when it happened, either."

"I doona wish to argue with ye, lass. Let me take ye to where ye're staying—"

"I was staying at the Best Western." She pointed across the river to an empty bank. "It's not there."

He had no idea what a best western was, but if she had nowhere to go, it presented another dilemma. "These friends of yours…Do ye ken where they are?"

"In the twenty-first century, I suppose." Her voice quivered. "I am telling you the truth. I swear it. Somehow, I travelled through Time. I don't know how, and…" She gulped and began to shake. "…and I don't know how to get back."

His first reaction was to take her into his arms and hold her close, but he was afraid she'd bolt. The last thing he needed was for the lass to go running off into the darkness of night all alone. He did reach for her hand, though. Thankfully, she didn't pull away. He gave it a light squeeze.

"Doona fash. At least, nae for tonight. If ye'll trust me, I will take ye to my home and we can sort this out in the morning."

Her eyes widened. "I just met you. Do you really expect me to walk off into the night with you?"

He didn't blame her for asking the question, although it did sting a little. He dropped her hand. "What other plan do ye have?"

She looked around and pointed. "I could curl up over there by one of the store entrances."

He frowned at her. "Either ye are daft or ye think I am."

"I don't think you're daft. It's just that… You are a stranger."

"I am a Stuart. My clan would disown me if I left ye here alone."

"Well, I'm not sure…"

"I give ye my word. Nae only as a Stuart, but as a Highlander. Nae harm will come to ye under my protection."

He watched her as Thea looked around as if trying to weigh her options. The cobblestoned street was empty, the shops along the way dark. There really was no place for her to go. The few inns that Inverness had would be full with the revelers coming in from all over the countryside. Ian remained silent, though, letting her come to that conclusion herself.

Finally, she turned to him. "Do you live far from here?"

That answer could be a yes or a no, depending on how familiar she was with the area and what her definition of "far" meant. "I live at Kilcoy Castle on the Black Isle. 'Tis a fair distance by road, but much closer by boat."

"Boat?"

"Aye. We've a small sailing ship moored, waiting for the tide to turn." He glanced up at the full moon. "We have about an hour."

"I can't just sail off into nowhere with you!"

He sighed. "If ye doona think ye can trust me, then I'll stay here with ye until dawn."

She gave him a wide-eyed look. "You would do that?"

"I canna leave ye here by yourself."

"Yes, you could. I will manage…"

"Nae.." He tugged her hand inside his arm. "Then we will spend the night at one of the storefronts." He raised his other hand to hush her protests. "'Tis my final word. I willna leave ye alone, lass."

****

I willna leave ye alone, lass. The words had rung over and over in her mind as they'd found a storefront that had an indentation to its door which offered a little bit of protection against the wind and cold. Ian had roused the street urchin who'd been using it, given him a coin—along with instructions to go to his boat and tell the crew to leave and return in the morning—and then told her to curl up inside the entry. He'd given her his coat to use as a blanket while he sat with his back against the wall, his sword across his lap, and told her to get some sleep.

She hadn't noticed the sword before. Perhaps it was that—he was guarding her—or that he was sitting in the cold without a jacket, it didn't take her long to decide to trust him to take her to his home. And so they'd gone to the docks.

Thea looked up at him now, leaning against the port side rail of the boat as the sun's first rays began to lighten the sky behind them. "Is it much farther?"

"Nae. Another fifteen or twenty minutes and we'll be docked."

"I'm glad to hear it."

Ian frowned. "Are ye feeling ill?"

"It's not that." Actually, she was an experienced sailor, thanks to her parents and their ancestral Nordic love for the sea. "I think your crew will be glad once I'm off their ship."

His frown deepened. "I doubt any of them think having a woman aboard is bad luck, lass."

"I'm not so sure."

"Doona fash. We'll soon have the boat tied."

The sooner, the better. The journey, which should have taken no more than an hour, had stretched into well over two, and she suspected some of the crew blamed her for the problems.

At first, she'd breathed a sigh of relief that the boat was still at the pier last night, but it didn't take long to realize the sailors weren't happy with the late departure. Evidently, the urchin had not delivered the message and they'd been waiting for Ian to show up. That meant the tide was already well out and they scraped bottom several times, having to pole themselves off before reaching deep enough water to sail. Then the rudder had locked, probably stuck with mud, which meant a man had to go overboard and clean it. Even though he'd been fully clothed, with a rope secured around him for retrieval, the temperature of the water had him near hypothermia when he got back on board. As they were hoisting the jib, a sheet snapped, which meant the foresail couldn't be used. And the mainsail, used more for stability than forward thrust, started luffing when the wind died. They were doing the sailing equivalent of limping home with two sprained ankles.

"Still, I'll bet your men will let me be the first one off," Thea said and then added, "I've gotten a number of less-than-friendly looks, in case you haven't noticed."

"'Tis nae matter. Look…" He pointed. "There's the Black Isle. We're home."

Thea looked at the horizon, where a thin line of black soil was beginning to loom larger as the boat finally approached a small inlet. Unlike nearby Inverness, which was covered in patches of snow, this land seemed to lack it, probably because it was surrounded by water on three sides. Whatever the reason, it lived up to its name, the Black Isle.

And it was to be her home for now.

Chapter Two

Thea had been right about being the first person to leave the boat. The lines had barely been secured when the short gangplank to the dock was lowered and the sailor indicated with a wave of his hand that she should descend, and he quickly stepped back.

Ian hid his irritation with the man for not stepping off first to help her. Before he could do so himself, she agilely hopped down, landing with a graceful balance that showed no semblance of needing to find her land legs. The sailor took another step backward and looked furtively around. Ian sighed. He'd seen the startled glances that the crew had given Thea when they boarded. Her hair had come undone sometime earlier and flowed around her shoulders like pale sea mist, her eyes almost the same color in the dim light. He'd heard murmurings about a water wraith and a couple of men had even covertly made the sign of the cross. Even though this was the mid-eighteenth century, it seemed there still were superstitious sailors. He didn't suppose all the little incidents along the way helped any. At least, they were now on solid ground.

"How far is the castle?" Thea asked as they started up a path leading away from the water.

"Just past this hillock. Ye'll be able to see it in a minute."

"Are you sure your family won't think me an

imposition? I'm a total stranger…" She paused. "…and not from here."

To avoid getting into that discussion again, he simply replied, "'Tis the Highlander way to offer hospitality, lass." The idea that she was from a different century—the future, no less—simply wasn't possible. Although she acted and sounded quite normal, she did say she was named for a Greek goddess. That, along with her wondering where the lights and the building had gone in Inverness made him fear she might be touched in the head. His own head was aching after having no sleep, and he was too tired to think straight. But he needed to clarify a few things before they reached the castle.

"Kilcoy Castle is nae my home—"

"You're taking me to total strangers?" Thea cut in. "You don't live here?"

"Nae. Well, aye." He shook his head more to clear it than emphasize his response. "What I mean is, I'm living here temporarily. My home is Stalker Castle in Appin."

Her brow crinkled. "Isn't that on the west side of Scotland?" He started to nod and she continued, "Why are you here, then? Please explain."

"I'm trying to, lass." He wished she'd let him explain. Usually, he didn't mind being asked questions, but his own brain was feeling a bit frazzled.

"I'm sorry. I didn't mean to interrupt."

Thea suddenly looked crestfallen and he felt like a dolt. "Nae. 'Twas rude of me to say that."

She started to open her mouth and then clamped it shut, chewing her lip. That made him think about how very kissable her mouth was. He shook his head again.

He really needed to concentrate.

"Kilcoy Castle was originally a Stuart holding but is now owned by the Mackenzies, specifically George Mackenzie, who is a general in the Jacobite army. He's away with the bonnie prince. We're currently using the place to bring wounded men to recover—"

"That's wonderful!" Thea obviously forgot she wasn't going to interrupt. "I have a little experience with healing, so I can help."

He gave her a dubious look, not sure he wanted to know exactly what she meant. He certainly wasn't in any state of mind to contend with some futuristic idea of medical practices. "'Tis kind of ye, but we have a full-time surgeon on premises. In addition," he went on quickly before she could protest, "My cousin, Charles Stuart of Ardsheal, is in command of the castle and the troops."

"Troops? You mean to send them back to war?"

Ian nodded. "When they're well enough, but we also get new recruits ready to answer the prince's call. I'm their trainer."

Thea gave him a sharp look. "You prepare men to go to war?"

"Well, aye." He felt confused. "To put the prince back on the throne, we have to fight."

"Violence is not the answer."

He raised a brow. "Do ye think old George will simply hand over the crown?"

"No. He won't. But..." She stopped, chewing her lip again.

He tried to avoid the temptation. "But what?"

"But..." She hesitated, as if thinking what she wanted to say. Then she shook her head. "...it's just that too many people die in war." She lifted her chin. "And that's not necessary."

Ian started to reply, then thought better of it. It would take a lot longer than he had right now to explain why it was necessary to put a Stuart back on the throne. That conversation could wait. He just hoped she wasn't going to side with the English government. He rubbed his temple where a headache was threatening to develop. He didn't need to be inventing a problem that might not exist. At least, he hoped it didn't.

"Look," he said, changing the subject as they passed the hillock and he stopped. "There's the castle. What do ye think?"

****

What she thought was that Ian hadn't wanted to respond to her statement. It actually was better that he hadn't. She had been about to tell him Scotland was going to lose this war, but—given he was a military trainer—he obviously wouldn't agree. Worse, he'd most likely think her completely mad and have her locked away somewhere. She couldn't risk that.

She turned her attention to the castle. In the early morning sunshine, the stones had a pinkish tint and it was massive, rising five stories with a pair of round towers at opposite corners. The roof was gray slate with crow-stepped gables, dormer windows and—she squinted—gun loops. It seemed more of a fortress than a home, but then, that's what castles were. Even the numerous steps leading to the front doors were built into what had been layered banks—another defensive strategy to make it harder for an enemy to charge the walls.

"Well?"

Thea started, realizing Ian was waiting for an

answer. "It's huge. How old is it?"

"It was started by the Stuarts in 1580 and completed in 1618 by the Mackenzies after they'd married into the family."

"It's hard to believe something that old is still in such good condition."

Ian drew his brows together. "'Tis only one hundred twenty-eight years. There are plenty castles about older than this one."

"That's ancient where I come from." Thea bit her lip as a wary expression crossed his face.

"Before we go inside…" He paused. "…mayhap we need to talk."

"About?" It wasn't a necessary question since Thea felt fairly certain she knew the answer, but she wanted to know what he was really thinking.

"About where ye are from…where ye say ye are from," he clarified.

"I know you don't believe me. I don't blame you," she added quickly. "I wouldn't believe it either if someone told me they were from the future—or the past, for that matter, since that's where I am—" She shook her head. She was babbling. "I digress." She sighed. "But what I told you was true. I live in the United States of America except, of course, it's the English Colonies right now and isn't in existence yet…" Good lord. She was babbling again. "…but it's there in the twenty-first century." From his incredulous look, she knew she should stop, but she might as well finish. She lifted her chin. "I am from the twenty-first century."

The incredulity changed to wariness again and she couldn't blame Ian for that either. Not only was she making outlandish statements, but she was practically gibbering. If she weren't careful, she'd be walking into that castle as a prisoner or, at least, someone who needed to be confined until appropriate action could be taken. She took a deep breath. "Whatever else you might think, please, please believe me when I say I am quite sane."

His wolf-colored eyes studied her silently, and she tried not to flinch. She wasn't going to act like helpless prey. She lifted her head high. "You might as well tell me what you think."

Ian kept silent a moment longer. "I am nae sure what I think right now, but I ken we need to tell a story that's believable when we go into the castle."

We? He'd said we? Ian was going to help her? Relief spread over her like warm shower water. She could take her time in convincing him she spoke the truth. Right now, inventing a plausible story made sense.

"What do you have in mind?"

He tilted his head. "Ye are a Ross. Two of the chieftain's sons are here at Kilcoy. We will say ye are kin from the Colonies…" He gave her a stern look. "…and ye'd planned to book a ferry to the Black Isle, but I offered to bring ye." He frowned. "There are a lot of loopholes I doona like, but 'tis credible." His look intensified again. "Ye will have to play your part."

Thea had never considered acting to be any part of her skill set, but she understood the need for it. Her explanation of travelling through time wasn't plausible, even if it were true. She certainly didn't want to end up in an eighteenth-century version of a madhouse. Women in this century had no rights anyway…a point she definitely needed to remember. Maybe she could picture herself as one of Charlotte's heroines and get through this. An idea began to glimmer in her mind.

"Well?"

Ian was waiting for an answer. Again. She really needed to stop drifting off or he'd lose whatever belief he had in her too.

"I think I have a better story."

He raised a brow. "And it is?"

The idea started launching itself. Maybe some of Charlotte's writing skills—plotting skills anyhow—had rubbed off.

"Instead of me being from the Colonies, let's say I'm from Nova Scotia. It's more believable since Scots settled there. My mother's parents were MacDonalds who actually did live there." She gave him a big smile. "And this isn't even a lie. My parents have a summer cabin in Halifax since the heat and humidity is awful in Texas."

He drew his brows together. "We canna talk about this Texas place."

"Okay, then. Just say my parents live in Nova Scotia."

"Hmmm." He considered. "I suppose that might work."

"Fine. Then that's settled."

He didn't look like anything was fine or settled, but she wasn't going to argue.

"Shall we proceed, then?"

He took a deep breath. "Aye. We'll proceed."

****

Before they'd reached the final steps, the door was flung open. Thea assumed their approach had been watched, and with great anticipation, at least by the dark-haired girl who practically flew out and latched onto Ian's arm.

"Ye are home! We thought ye were following us last night, but when we got here, ye were nae in sight!"

"I was delayed a bit." Ian extricated his arm from her grip and gestured. "I've brought a guest."

The girl, who appeared to be in her late teens, turned her gaze to Thea. She narrowed her dark eyes slightly before turning back to Ian. "So who is this?"

This, Thea wanted to say, was a person, not an object, and could be addressed directly, but she held her peace. It wasn't like her to feel instant irritation. Charlotte and Vi would probably tease about her "preternatural" instincts, but something about the girl was off-putting. She hoped the girl wasn't Ian's sister or, worse, his wife.

"This is Athena Ross," he replied and then turned to Thea. "This is Cora Chattan, our surgeon's daughter."

"Hello, Cora." Not a sister or a wife, then. Did Ian have a wife? She hadn't thought about that. The thought was a bit disturbing, although she didn't know why it should be. Maybe because they'd kissed. She certainly didn't make a habit of kissing married men. In truth, she didn't make a habit of kissing any longer at all.

"Why is she here?"

Thea frowned slightly. Cora hadn't replied to her greeting, and now she was asking Ian the question like Thea wasn't standing right there. Her feeling of annoyance grew.

"Miss Ross is distant kin of Malcolm and John—"

"Are ye going to stand outside until icicles form in the doorway?" Another female voice interrupted them.

This one sounded friendly, though, and when she stepped out, she had a smile on her face. She looked to be in her twenties, with auburn hair and green eyes that looked a bit mischievous. Thea instantly warmed toward her. And also to the black cat that came out and wrapped herself against Thea's legs. She reached down to pet it and evoking a large purr.

"That's Edie." The girl looked a bit puzzled. "It's surprising she came out into the cold, but come inside, the lot of ye, before Mrs. Moffat serves us dry bread and water for our next meal because we're letting the whole floor cool off." She turned to Cora. "Your father is looking for ye."

"Mrs. Moffat is the housekeeper," Ian told Thea as Cora left and the three of them—and the cat—moved inside. "She'd make a good general if the prince would let her into the army."

"True enough," the girl said. "Maybe I should talk to my uncle about it?"

"Your uncle wouldna let his best employee leave," Ian answered and turned to Thea. "May I introduce Moire Mackenzie, niece of General George Mackenzie." He shifted to Moire. "This is Athena Ross."

"Ross?" Moire's eyes twinkled. "Are ye a hostage too?"

Thea blinked. "Hostage?"

"Doona be scaring the lass," Ian said. "Besides, ye are nae a hostage."

"Strictly speaking, I am." Moire looked at Thea, obviously not about to stop. "My father is Kenneth Mackenzie, brother of the general. He supports the English, though. My uncle figures my father will leave Kilcoy Castle alone if I'm kept here." She made a face at Ian. "Which makes me a hostage."

"One who has every demand met," Ian countered.

Clearly, the two of them had an easygoing

relationship and Moire was not in danger of being treated like a prisoner. Thea recalled that it hadn't been that uncommon in more medieval times for chieftains to foster their offspring with rivals to ensure peace was kept. Maybe the concept should be revisited in more modern times, given the turmoil unleashed in her century.

But she wasn't in her century. She still couldn't fathom how she'd managed to time-travel, but she felt strangely calm. Alan, gentle soul that he'd been, always said everyone was where they needed to be at the moment they were there. Young as they'd been, it had been an easy concept to accept, at least until he'd been killed so senselessly. After his death, she'd struggled to come to terms with what happened.

Maybe that was why she was here. Maybe, in this moment, given that she knew the future, she could change it. She'd wanted to research the Stuarts and the futile, final claim they made for the throne. Maybe she could prevent more senseless violence from happening. The Jacobites were not only going to lose the war to the English, they were going to be massacred at the battle of Culloden.

Unless the battle didn't happen.

Maybe that was why she was here.

Chapter Three

"So who is the bonny lass ye brought home?"

Even though he'd been preparing for the question most of the day, Ian still nearly choked on the sip of whisky he'd just taken. Forcing himself to swallow carefully, he put the glass down on the small table between the two armchairs in the study in which he and his cousin, Charles Stuart of Ardsheal, were sitting in front of a crackling fire. Although the question had been asked in the most neutral of tones, the penetrating look he was getting meant he wasn't going to be allowed to give a neutral answer.

Not only was his cousin known to be one of the best swordsman in Scotland—he'd even wounded Rob Roy Macgregor once—but his ability to discern when someone was lying was another reason General Mackenzie had given Charles command of the troops at Kilcoy Castle.

"I met her at the Hogmanay dance," he replied, not adding the quite intimate way they had met. He could still feel Thea's soft, warm lips against his… Ian pushed the thought aside, hoping Charles wouldn't sense a personal interest. His cousin was more of an older brother to him since Ian had lived with Charles's family after his own father was killed in the 1715 Uprising. He'd been but a bairn and Charles had been fifteen. There had been several instances, in his adolescent years, when Charles had to rescue him from potential parsons' nooses. Better not let him think this was another one.

"I doona ken much about her other than her friends seemed to have deserted her." He didn't mention that supposedly they were in the twenty-first century. "She had nae place to go, and I couldna leave her alone in the middle of the night in the cold."

"Understandable."

Again, the tone was neutral, conveying nothing of Charles' thoughts, but his expression was alert. "Did the lass tell ye where she is from?"

Ah. That was the question he'd been preparing an answer for. "The lass is from Nova Scotia."

"What is she doing here?"

"She married a Scot. Unforunately, he was killed shortly after they came back." Thea had told him last night as they were sailing that she was a widow. It had been a shock, but she didn't seem to want to talk about it and he hadn't pressed.

"So what was she doing in Inverness?"

"I think she had plans to try and get back to Nova Scotia, but her escort made off with her belongings and money." This was a bit of invention he'd added to make the whole story more plausible. "She is destitute, but her last name is Ross, so maybe Malcolm or John might be of help."

"Except that neither one of them is here right now. I sent Malcolm down to Bannockburn to consult with the prince, and John is out recruiting more troops for the Cause."

Ian hid his disappointment. Since Thea couldn't be from the twenty-first century, he'd hoped either Malcolm or John could actually identify her as part of their clan and he'd find out what secret she was really hiding.

"So we doona ken whether she is a Jacobite or supports King George?"

"Nae."

"Mmmm. Then ye will need to keep an eye on her."

"Aye, I will." Ian bit his lip to keep from smiling. His cousin had no idea how gladly he'd keep an eye on Thea. A widow out of widow's weeds might even welcome the attention. Based on how she kissed... He shut the thought down. Now was not the time to think about that. When he'd asked Thea about her stance, she'd said violence wasn't the answer, but that wasn't definitive. It was important to know which side she favored, but anyone could lie to protect themselves. He already suspected, based on vague responses to his questions on the boat, that Thea was quite good at protecting herself, as though she had an invisible cloak to wrap around her thoughts and feelings. Maybe he only sensed that because he kept a wall around his own emotions. But there were more subtle ways of finding out if she were a Jacobite besides asking.

There were a lot of things he wanted to find out about Thea Ross, and he would take his time finding the answers.

****

"This is quite impressive," Thea said to Moire as they entered the Great Hall that afternoon. Even though she was tired from lack of sleep—and hopping from one century to another—she was curious about the castle. When Moire had offered to give her a tour, she eagerly said yes. Edie, the cat, had decided to take the tour with them.

"She either really likes ye or she's hungry for a

mouse," Moire said.

"Let's hope it's the first," Thea answered. "Not that I'm fond of mice, but I'd hate to see one killed in front of me. It would make me think Edie is a bad cat." The cat meowed at her as though she understood, and Thea laughed and picked her up as she followed Moire. "I didn't mean to insult you, sweetie."

"This is where the men who are in training eat their meals," Moire said as they entered a huge room.

Thea craned her neck to look around. It was a medieval Great Hall. At the far end was a dais with a wide hearth behind it to keep the honored guests seated at the high table warm and toasty on cold, drafty nights. The Mackenzie Coat of Arms hung above it. Several smaller hearths lined each side of the rectangular room to keep the occupants on the benches of the long trestle tables warm as well. A rather intimidating number of swords and shields were mounted on the walls, along with a lot of empty hooks. "It looks rather like an armory."

"It *is* an armory of sorts. Weapons always need to be ready at hand, but…" Moire replied, "…'tis hard for soldiers to sit and eat with their swords attached. Especially those…" She pointed to an area where huge Scottish claymores hung. "Weapons always need to be handy."

Thea knew that the claymores were generally worn across the back since they were too long to dangle off a belt. "Actually, I think those could be used as backrests for the benches."

Moire laughed. "That's an idea that hasn't been tried. I'll have to let the earl know."

"Earl?"

"My uncle George. Besides being a general, he's the Earl of Cromartie."

Thea had almost forgotten that Scots held aristocratic titles as well as the English. Maybe she was actually in the presence of a Lady Moire. "Does your father have a title too?"

"Aye. He's Lord Fortrose of Inverness Burghs."

She was in the presence of a lady. Too bad Charlotte wasn't here. She'd be thrilled. But Thea didn't want to offend her newfound friend in this century. "Is it all right for me to call you just 'Moire'?"

"Och, aye! We doona stand on formality here." She grinned. "'Twould be too English, ye ken."

Thea grinned back and then let the smile fade. "I don't understand, though, how your father and your uncle can be on opposite sides of this war. They're brothers."

Moire shrugged. "'Tis nae that uncommon. The Duke of Atholl defends Blair Castle for the English. His brother is General George Murray, who supports the prince. "'Tis the same with the Grants. Colonel James Grant holds command in the Jacobite army while his brother, Major George Grant, supports King George."

"Lots of Georges, aren't there?"

Moire laughed again. "It does seem that both sides are fond of the name."

Britain would have a few more, including a future one in her century. Thea let the thought pass. Best not to dwell on the future until she had time to think things through.

"I guess you don't know if there are any sisterly conflicts since women aren't allowed to be generals or colonels or majors."

Moire's eyes twinkled. "Well, we do have Lady Anne MacKintosh. The prince made her a colonel after she personally recruited nearly four hundred men for him. Her husband is a captain in the king's Black Watch."

"Maybe more women should be made officers. We could end this war."

A confused expression crossed Moire's face. "But who would win?"

"Nobody. Everybody." Thea waved a hand. "You could just live in peace."

Moire looked around and then lowered her voice. "'Twould be best if ye doona say that when anyone is around. 'Twould seem traitorous."

Traitorous. Good lord! If that's what they would think, she'd be tossed out on her ear—or worse. "I didn't mean it like that. Please believe me. I just meant it would be good to prevent bloodshed."

Moire nodded. "'Twould be good, but Scotland has been under English rule for too long. Now a king from Prussia reigns. Ian and his cousin are determined that a Stuart take the throne again."

That wasn't going to happen. Not in this century at least. There was a man in her century who'd been born in Belgium but claimed to be a descendent of Charles Edward Stuart through an illegitimate daughter the prince had not yet fathered. That claim had gone nowhere either. Modern-day Scotland had promptly revoked his passport. Not that any of that mattered except for the sad irony of it all.

"I probably need to learn more about this whole situation. I...I've been out of the country for quite a while." That was certainly true.

Moire drew her brows together. "How long have ye been away?"

Over two hundred and fifty years? Thea couldn't give that answer. "Ah…my husband died three years ago and I decided to travel." That was basically true. Alan had been gone three years and she had travelled to Greece a year ago and now she'd come to Scotland…just that it had all happened in another century.

Moire's expression cleared. "That explains it, then. Ye were nae here when word about the Cause started circulating nor when the prince arrived last summer."

Thea mentally grabbed that thread as though it were a lifeline in a churning sea. "Yes. Please forgive me if I speak out of turn. I understand now that I need to learn more."

"Aye." Moire's eyes twinkled again. "I'm sure Ian will be glad to teach ye."

What did that comment mean? Had Moire not believed their explanation of her being stranded at Hogmanay? Or did she think something had happened between them? Warmth spread across her face and Thea hoped she wasn't blushing furiously. Something had happened. A very thorough kiss that she could still feel had happened. She had returned it with equal fervor while straddling the man, no less. That was quite unexpected, since her marriage had been quietly conventional.

A thought suddenly flashed through her mind that had nothing to do with Ian schooling her on the Jacobite cause, but everything to do with what else he could teach her. Her face flamed.

She was most definitely blushing.

****

Thea was relieved to find out that the "family" took their evening meal in a smaller room across from the kitchens rather than in the massive Great Hall. It had been a tiring day and her lack of sleep was rapidly kicking in. She wasn't sure she was up to being scrutinized by more than a hundred troops eating in the same room.

Not that she wasn't without scrutinizing in this room. The large dining table was round which, in King Arthur's time, meant all his knights were equal, but in this instance really meant everyone was able to see each other. Three places next to her were still empty but once they were taken, she'd more than likely be the center of attention, a position she didn't particularly like, instead of being seated at the far end of a table where she might retreat into relative obscurity. At least Moire sat on her other side. They'd had a chance to get better acquainted while she was being shown around this afternoon, and she'd felt an affinity.

"Have a bannock while we're waiting." Moire held up a plate with the delicious smelling bread rolls.

Thea took one. "They're still warm!"

"Aye. 'Tis why we eat close to the kitchen," Ian grinned. "Food tastes better that way."

She'd tried not to stare at him when he'd come in, but her stomach fluttered a little bit anyhow. She hadn't seen him since early this morning when they'd docked, and she didn't want to appear eager or, worse, desperate for his attention. He'd traded his kilt for tight-fitting breeches that outlined his muscular legs, and his white shirt, open at the collar, had the sleeves rolled up, exposing powerful forearms. Obviously, dressing for dinner was not a necessity.

He'd taken a seat across from her, and Cora, the surgeon's daughter, had quickly slipped into the chair beside him. Her father sat next to her. He had the same dark hair and eyes as his daughter. Thea got the distinct impression he was studying her much like he might a specimen under a microscope. She tried not to squirm. She wanted to work with this man. Alan had been getting ready for a medical internship when he was killed, and she'd helped him study for exams, so she should be able to help with some of the wounded soldiers that came in.

Thea started to ask him what hours he kept, but the door opened again . The man who stepped inside practically oozed authority, from his military stance to his stern-looking face. He was also powerfully built. She'd thought Ian muscular—and he was—but this man looked like he could easily throw a twenty-foot, one-hundred-fifty-pound caper at the Highland Games with little effort. To her consternation, he took the seat next to her.

"I'm Charles Ardsheal." He gave her a curt nod. "Ye must be Miss Ross?"

She swallowed, thankful she hadn't taken a bite of bread. Even his voice was commanding. "Yes. I…I understand you are in charge here?"

"Aye. Until Cromartie comes back."

"Which willna be for a while, if what the soldiers say is true," the surgeon said.

Ardsheal diverted his attention. "Did someone bring news?"

The man nodded. "Two brought supplies in this afternoon. The word is Hawley is marching the Redcoats toward Stirling to relieve the siege."

He frowned. "The prince is nae far from there at

Bannockburn."

"And Cromartie is in Derby now," Ian said. "At least, that's the last information I got."

"Aye," Ardsheal said, "but hopefully he'll be heading back north soon with a number of new troops."

"I hope Murray has lookouts posted so he can warn Cromartie," Ian replied.

"So do I." Ardsheal stood and motioned to Ian. "Let's retreat to the study. We can have trays sent in."

Ian pushed back his chair as well and turned to Thea. "I'd hoped to talk to ye, lass, but it will have to wait until tomorrow."

Thea nodded, but her head was spinning. The men had just been talking about the upcoming battle that would take place at Falkirk in a couple of weeks. Should she say something? If she recalled correctly, this was a Scottish victory. Maybe she should hold her tongue until she was more sure of her footing. But…could bloodshed be prevented? Would there be injuries or would it be a rout? Right now, her brain was too tired to remember the details. Ian had said they'd talk tomorrow.

She would have to wait. For now.

****

The next morning after they'd broken their fast and everyone was leaving the room, Ian asked Thea, "Would ye stay a minute? I'd like to talk." She'd started to get up, but sat down, giving him a wary look.

"Of course."

He wasn't sure where he wanted to start. Yesterday had been hectic and, with the news that the English general was marching toward Stirling, he'd been in deep discussion with Charles on what preparations they'd need to make. That news had also taken Ardsheal's mind off Thea's unexpected—and strange—arrival, but Ian knew his cousin would be returning to the matter soon. He sighed.

"I was hoping that either Malcolm or John would be here. 'Tis a shame they're gone."

"Why?"

"They're Rosses." He frowned. "I told ye that."

"You did." She frowned too. "What difference does that make?"

Ian lifted a brow. "They are your kin, remember?"

Thea scoffed. "That's not an excuse—"

"Did I say it was an excuse?"

Her brows drew together again. "What do you mean by that?"

"I mean that one of them might ken who ye are."

She shook her head. "They won't know me because I'm from the future."

"'Tis impossible."

"But it's true."

Ian wasn't sure if she was being deliberately obtuse or genuinely confused. He wasn't sure which was worse, either. If she were deliberately being stubborn, she might be hiding something that could be dangerous to the people here at Kilcoy. If she were truly confused, then there might be something wrong with her. He remembered a lass at Appin that believed she was one of Henry VIII's wives and that he was looking for her. The poor lass was finally taken to a sanatorium in Glasgow. His cousin would certainly remember the whole thing, as well. Ian didn't want Thea being sent anywhere.

"Ye canna keep saying that. 'Tis dangerous."

She opened her mouth to retort, then must have thought better of it since she started chewing her lip. It was a nervous move on her part, but it nearly drove him mad with desire. He wanted nothing more than to clamp his mouth over hers and kiss her senseless. *Eejit.*

"I suppose you're right. I'll not mention it again in front of anyone. However…" She paused and tilted her head to one side, studying him.

"What?" he asked. "Finish, please."

"I want you to believe me. If I can predict the future outcome of Falkirk, would you believe me then?"

"Falkirk?"

"That's where the next battle will be. The one with General Hawley."

Ian shook his head. "He is marching on Stirling to break the siege there."

"That's probably the original plan," Thea replied, "but he'll be intercepted." She frowned. "According to the history books, Ardsheal should be at the battle."

"There ye go, then. My uncle is here." Ian smirked a little. "Or do ye think he can be in two places at once?"

She gave him an annoyed look. "Of course not. That's impossible."

He raised a brow. "But ye think travelling through Time isna?"

"I already told you I don't know how that happened." She sighed. "But it did. That's how I know the battle at Falkirk will take place."

In spite of himself, he asked, "Who wins?"

"Ultimately, the Jacobites, but there will be confusion on both sides and there will be failure to follow through."

He started to ask what she meant by that, but stopped himself. This conversation was ridiculous. He shouldn't even have asked the first question. Thea couldn't know how a battle—that wasn't even projected to happen— would end. There was no point in encouraging any such talk.

"If it will help you to believe me, the battle will happen on January seventeenth. Your cousin Ardsheal is supposed to be there."

"Enough, lass! We'll nae talk about this anymore." He pushed his chair back and stood. As he did so, he heard a slight noise outside the door. He reached it in three strides and looked out.

"What is it?" Thea asked, coming to his side. "Is someone there?"

He shook his head. "I thought I heard something, but everything is clear."

'Well, then, I suppose I should find Moire. She promised to finish showing me around."

"Aye. And I need to get started with my day as well." He paused before leaving. "Remember what I said. Nae talk of the future."

Thea grimaced. "I'll remember."

****

Cora scurried around the corner and flattened herself against the wall as she listened to footsteps going in the other direction. Thankfully, she hadn't been caught eavesdropping.

She didn't like the woman Ian had brought home. And what had she meant that she was from the future?

Chapter Four

"I will have to do something to reimburse you for all of these purchases," Thea said to Moire the next day as they concluded a shopping spree in Inverness.

"Nonsense. I have plenty of funds since my father made sure accounts were set up for me once I became Uncle George's hostage."

"Will ye stop saying ye are a hostage?" Ian asked in an exasperated tone. "Ye'll have Thea believing it."

Moire wrinkled her nose at him. "Uncle George gave strict orders that I was to go nowhere unescorted, not even on a ride around his own property. What else would ye call it?"

"I would call it common sense," Ian answered. "In case ye missed it, we've got hundreds of men coming and going for training up here. The earl canna vouch that they are all honorable. Do ye want to start an inner-clan war between your father and uncle when we've a more important one right now?"

"They are already on different sides, ye ken," Moire replied dryly.

"I ken, but they are nae threatening to kill each other." Ian scowled at her. "Which might verra well be the case if something happens to ye."

"I think Ian might have a point," Thea interrupted. Unfortunately, women alone were vulnerable, much as she hated to admit it. "Even if you weren't harmed, getting accosted would be frightening."

Moire clamped a hand over her mouth and reached out to her with the other one. "I'm sorry. I forgot that ye were just robbed."

Thea hated lying, but they had decided her "escort" had ridden off with her worldly goods. "Well—"

"Aye," Ian cut in and gave Moire a stern look. "And that was by someone Thea thought she could trust. We doona ken who all the men are that are in these parts these days."

"All right. All right. Ye've made your point." Moire didn't look particularly repentant. "It doesna mean that I am nae a hostage, though."

Perhaps it was time to change the subject since Thea was beginning to suspect that both of them were going to become mulish. "Perhaps we could stroll a bit by the river?"

"Aye. We've got a bit of time before the tide turns," Ian said. "I'll be happy to escort ye."

Moire glanced from one of them to the other and Thea thought she saw a mischievous spark in her eyes. "I just remembered there was another bonnet I wanted to buy. I can meet ye by back here in half an hour."

Thea felt her face warm. It seemed rather obvious that Moire was giving them time to be alone. Not that she minded being alone with him—she'd admit she was attracted to him—but she didn't want Ian thinking she had set him up. Truthfully, though, she had a another reason for wanting to be alone with him and it didn't have anything to do with romantic inclinations.

She wanted him—them—to revisit the place where he'd fallen and she'd touched him and ended up in the eighteenth century.

Ian tucked her hand into the bend of his elbow after Moire had crossed the street, heading for a shop. "So where would ye like to walk?"

Thea could feel the strength of his forearm even though her fingers were resting lightly on his sleeve. His biceps flexed as he moved his arm to a better position and for a moment she was totally distracted. Although Alan had been trim and fit, he was a scholarly sort, not given to workouts in a gym. The power of Ian's muscles fascinated her and she resisted the urge to wrap her fingers around as much of his arm as she could.

"Lass?"

Thea pulled herself back to reality. She really needed to stop letting her thoughts wander off into fantasy land. She was pretty sure women in this century didn't just let their hands roam all over a man's body. Where had that urge come from anyway?

"Lass?" he asked again.

She blinked. She really needed to stop thinking along those lines. "Actually, I wanted to go to the spot where you fell at Hogmanay."

He gave her a cautious look. "Why?"

"I…was thinking that maybe I could find a clue."

His expression turned wary. "What kind of clue?"

"As to how I may have gotten here. Maybe there's a time portal or something."

He turned, disengaging his arm and putting both hands on her shoulders. "Athena. Ye have got to stop talking like this. If anyone hears ye, they will think ye daft." He paused. "Or worse."

Thea looked around. "There's no one nearby."

Ian huffed in exasperation. "Ye are as difficult as Moire."

She frowned at him. "I'm not difficult at all. My friends always tell me I'm too laid-back."

His eyebrow rose. "Laid back?"

Her face warmed. That hadn't come out exactly right. Ian was probably taking the term literally. "It means calm and easygoing."

"Easygoing?"

The heat intensified. Easy wasn't the right term either. "It means I am not difficult."

"Then why do ye keep pursuing this notion of being from the future?"

This time she gave the exasperated huff. "Because I *am* from the future."

"'Tis impossible."

"You keep saying that."

"Because I am right."

"You aren't." She held up a hand as he started to retort. "This conversation isn't going anywhere. Would you just please humor me and take me to the spot?"

He sighed. "Aye, then, if it will put an end to this talk."

"It might." As they started to walk, she added, "I sometimes can feel sensations that others don't—"

"It might be best if ye doona talk like that either," Ian said.

Thea looked heavenward. "It's a talent I've had since I was a child. If there *is* a portal…" She held up her hand again to stop his reply. "…I'm pretty sure I'll be able to sense it."

He didn't answer and, from the stoic expression on his face—similar to the ones of men sitting on benches in malls waiting for their wives to finish shopping—he obviously had decided to cease arguing.

They walked south past the shops toward the castle. When they neared the area where the circle dance had taken place, Thea slowed. She and Ian hadn't actually danced, but there might be a current of energy emanating from the place since it was the traditional spot that had been used for centuries. Ian stopped too.

"Well?"

She stood a moment, sensing nothing. She shook her head. "This isn't where you fell."

He pointed. "It was over there."

At least they agreed on that. There was a slight incline that she remembered climbing to get to him. She walked slowly up it, sending sensory feelers out. Nothing. Stopping on the spot where he'd lain, she closed her eyes and concentrated. Still nothing. Opening her eyes, she saw he was watching her.

"Would you mind lying down?"

One eyebrow shot up. "I'd look a bit foolish lying down on the ground in the middle of the day."

"It will just be for a minute. I want to re-enact what happened."

The other brow rose. "Ye want to climb on top of me?"

"Well, no. That wasn't at all what I what I had in mind—"

Ian grinned then. "Ye want to kiss me again?"

Thea felt herself blush. It seemed she wasn't good at explaining anything today. Not that she didn't want to kiss him. She could definitely recall that feeling and the sensation. She shook her head to clear it. She really had to concentrate on why she was here.

"Ye doona want to kiss me, then?"

"No. Yes. No…" She scowled at him when his grin

widened. He was teasing her and she was acting like a schoolgirl with a crush. "That's not what I meant."

He sobered. "Then what do ye mean?"

"I just want to kneel beside you and place my hand on your arm." She gestured to the ground where she'd found him. "That's when I felt this strange sensation of falling into nothingness…" She looked up at him. "…and awoke in your century."

He glanced down and then back to her. "If I do this, will ye promise to stop talking about being from the future?"

She paused, then nodded. If a reenactment didn't get a result—if there was no energy transfer—then she didn't know where else to turn.

"Do ye want me to stumble and fall or just lie down?"

She drew her brows together, not sure whether he was teasing her again or not. "Just lie down."

He slid effortlessly to the ground. She knelt beside him as she'd done before and touched his arm. For an instant, she relived the same moment at Hogmanay. Ian's hand flashed out, grabbing hers, and she found herself sprawled over his chest. Just like when— For a moment, she flashed back to Hogmanay, opening her eyes in this century and feeling his mouth on hers, his lips moving sensuously over hers, his arms holding her close, like he was doing now— She gave herself a shake. *Just like he was doing now?*

"What are you doing?"

"I'm recreating what happened." He grinned again, his hands loosely along her ribcage. "Should I kiss ye too?"

For a second, she wondered if he hadn't already

done that. The image had been so clear and it was tempting, but they were in the middle of the castle lawn in broad daylight. She became aware that they were already drawing onlookers, some of whom were smirking. She scrambled off him without answering, thankfully this time not getting caught up in her skirts. "You are incorrigible, sir!"

He shrugged, then sprang lightly to his feet. "I'm just doing what ye asked."

She supposed he was right, although she wasn't about to admit it. She just wanted to get out of public view. She hurried down the hill, Ian trailing after her.

It was only when she'd reached the relative safety of a semi-crowded street that she realized that, apart from the brief moment that had seemed like a time distortion, the only other sensation she'd felt was that of Ian's body pressed against hers.

There had been no portal.

****

As he followed Thea toward the shopping area, Ian tried to analyze what he knew about the lass. Applying logic to facts was what any good commander did when preparing for a battle. The problem was this was not exactly a battle, unless it was one of wills, and he had very few actual facts.

That he'd stumbled and fallen at Hogmanay was a fact. At the time he'd felt like someone had given him a hard push even though there had been no one around. He was sure of that. He wasn't as sure that he'd hit his head, but he must have since Athena had been sprawled over him and they were kissing when he opened his eyes. Those were definitely facts.

It was a little disturbing that he'd recalled—very

vividly—the whole episode as soon as she'd touched his arm just now. For a brief moment, the world had dissolved around him and he was only aware of Thea atop him again, warm and willing and compliant… He frowned. She hadn't been compliant at all. She'd practically thrown herself off him. He drew his brows closer together. He needed to curb his fanciful thoughts and stick to logic.

That she had come from someplace called Texas was not a fact. That she was from the twenty-first century was not a fact. He'd be barmy himself if he entertained those notions.

That left the question of who she really was. And, where had she come from?

In spite of the story they'd manufactured, how did she actually come to be in Inverness with no escort, no belongings, and no money? She'd said Malcolm and John wouldn't know her. Was that because she wasn't actually a Ross? If she wasn't a Ross, why would she use that surname when most of the clan supported the government? It would be far safer to claim to be a MacDonald if that was her grandfather's name. But maybe it wasn't. She was the one who came up with the idea that her parents were in Nova Scotia. It was common knowledge that masses of MacDonalds had immigrated there. He rubbed his temples. The facts were getting muddled.

"There ye are!" Moire came toward them, carrying several packages. "I was wondering when ye'd be back."

He was glad of the reprieve from his thoughts and looked at the bundles. "It seems ye bought more than just a bonnet."

"Well, ye weren't back, so I shopped some more."

"We havena been gone that long." He glanced at Thea, but she seemed to be lost in thought. He turned back to Moire. "We canna be more than five minutes late."

"Ye've been gone over an hour." She looked him over and grinned. "From the disarray of your clothes—nae to mention some blades of grass clinging to ye, I'll nae be asking ye what ye've been doing."

Thea blinked, coming out of her reverie. She turned slightly pink. "We weren't doing anything. Ian...slipped and fell on the grass near the castle."

"Did he now?" Moire gave Ian an arched look. "Was it the sight of ye slipping and falling that drew the crowd over there?"

The crowd. There had been an unusual number of people gathered there, now that he thought about it. The place had been empty when he and Thea had walked to it. There hadn't been anyone around when she'd asked him to lie down, either. Their enactment hadn't taken that long. How could a crowd have gathered in that short period?

But Moire said they'd been gone an hour. Thea hadn't challenged her. He shook his head. They couldn't have been gone that long. It wasn't possible. Time did not simply stand still, any more than it allowed someone to travel through it.

****

Thea wasn't sure what to make of the perplexed look on Ian's face as they walked toward their carriage. She was somewhat perplexed herself, although she doubted it was for the same reasons.

Why hadn't there been a portal? As vivid as the memory had just been of waking up in this century, she hadn't had the sensation of falling into nothingness like she'd done before. She had no idea if portals could move, but it seemed likely that it would be stationary. The only encounter she'd had with Ian—in the twenty-first century—had been on that exact same spot. She'd even gone through the same motions, although she must have taken longer than she'd thought, given that a small crowd had gathered and Moire said they'd been gone an hour. Strange, though. It hadn't seemed that long.

She glanced at Ian. His expression had changed and it now looked like a storm brewing. Moire must have noticed it too because she offered to go ahead and alert the coachman they were ready to leave.

"Are you angry with me?" Thea asked Ian once Moire was out of earshot.

He frowned. "Nae."

"You look upset." She wondered if maybe he felt insulted that she'd scrambled off him like she had after she'd been the one to ask him to lie down. "Are you sure?"

Ian's frown deepened. "I'm sure."

"Then why are you scowling?"

"I'm nae scowling."

"You are."

"Nae."

They were beginning to sound like children in a schoolyard. "All right. You're not scowling. You do look upset, though. Is it something I said or did?"

He stopped walking so abruptly she almost bumped against him. "What?"

He sighed. "'Tis everything ye say and do—"

"Well!" Her temper began to rise. "If everything I say or do irritates you, you should have said—"

"That isna what I meant." He held up a hand. "If ye'll let me finish?"

This time, she frowned. She did have a bad habit of jumping in and finishing someone's sentences. "All right."

"What I meant to say was that every time ye talk about being from the future, I doona ken what to make of it. Ye doona seem afflicted otherwise, but for that talk."

"I know it's hard to accept. I wouldn't believe me either except that it happened." She shook her head. "I don't know what else to say. I was hoping I'd sense something when we went back to the site, but nothing happened."

He scowled again. "Except that Moire says we spent more than an hour there. That's impossible too."

Thea hid her surprise. So he had felt a distortion of time too? She hadn't said anything when Moire said they'd been gone more than an hour because she hadn't wanted to deal with the innuendo of what they might have been doing.

But she wondered if maybe he'd been with her after all in that brief flashback—or flashforward—to the twenty-first century Hogmanay.

Chapter Five

Ian looked up from the desk as Moire poked her head inside the door to the library the next afternoon. "Do ye mind if we come in? I want to show Thea something."

"Aye, come in." Ian closed the ledger book he'd been working on, glad for a break. He'd been working on how to find additional monies to purchase some muskets so the entire Scottish army didn't have to rely on swords and targes. Cromartie's man-of-business, Elliott, had given him a tight budget to work with, and accounting wasn't his strong suit. He found working with numbers to be boring and, if things didn't balance when he finished, he generally invented a new curse word to use.

He rose and glanced at the row of figurines on the mantel. He had a pretty good idea what Moire wanted Thea to see.

"I wanted to bring ye in here the day I gave ye a tour of the castle, but Ian and Ardsheal were having a meeting," Moire said. "Heaven forbid that I interrupt some top-secret talk."

They'd actually been talking about Thea that day, so it was a good thing Moire hadn't bounced in. Not that he was going to point that out. "I didna think aspects of war strategies would interest ye."

"Aye, ye are right. 'Tis dull talk."

"I would be interested, though," Thea said.

Moire blinked in surprise while Ian studied her. "Why would ye want to listen to talk about war?"

Thea glanced at Moire before she answered. Ian hoped she wasn't going to mention something about future wars.

"The settlers in Nova Scotia have had disagreements with the native people. War is not always the answer."

Ian refrained from snorting. "Tell that to the Redcoats, lass."

"I would if I could." Thea gave him an arched look. "I am named after the goddess who protects soldiers, remember."

"Which is why I brought ye in here," Moire pointed to the figurines. "Those are all Greek gods and goddesses—Zeus, Hera, Apollo and you." She grinned. "I mean, Athena. And this one…" She indicated the remaining statue. "… Poseidon."

"I didn't know General Cromartie was interested in Greek history," Thea said.

Ian shrugged. "I'm nae sure he is. Those figurines have been passed down through several generations."

Thea walked closer to inspect them. "They're done in marble, just like the original ones at the Parthenon in Athens."

"Have ye been to Athens?" Moire asked.

"Actually, I did go there," she said. "It was…" Thea hesitated and Ian held his own breath hoping she wasn't going to say something nonsensical. "…after my husband was killed. I thought a change of scenery would be beneficial."

Ian released his breath. At least she hadn't said anything about travelling in the twenty-first century.

"I'm impressed." Moire plopped down in a chair. "Tell me about Athens."

Thea gave him a questioning look and he nodded, reluctantly. "Go ahead. Tell us what ye ken about ancient Athens." Hopefully, the lass would take the hint and not start talking about what it was like in the twenty-first century. Not that she would actually know. Why had that thought even entered his head? He must be going completely barmy to even entertain the idea.

"Well, if it's ancient Athens you want to know about, it does have an interesting mythical history," Thea said.

"Go on, then," Moire urged.

"There was a mythical king of Attica—the area where Athens now is—named Cecrops. He was half-man and half-snake, supposedly, and wanted to name the city Cecropia after himself, but the Olympian gods felt it should be named after one of them." Thea turned toward the statues on the mantel. "Athena and Poseidon were the major contenders."

"Were they related?" Moire asked.

Thea nodded. "Athena was the daughter of Zeus and Poseidon was her uncle." She smiled at Moire. "It sort of sounds like your situation only with your father being Poseidon and your uncle being Zeus."

"My uncle would probably like that comparison," Moire said.

Ian stifled a snort. "Better not let Prince Charlie hear one of his generals has been elevated to a god."

Thea looked serious. "Maybe that's been part of the problem. Wasn't the fact that the Stuart kings believed in the divine right of their ancestry—that they were above the law—that brought on the Glorious

Revolution?"

"Mayhap." Ian shrugged. "That doesna mean that our prince is nae the rightful heir to the throne, though. In fact—"

"Why are we talking about Prince Charlie?" Moire interrupted. "I want to hear about Athens."

Ian started to retort, then thought better of it. Whether the Stuart kings had the blessings of God wasn't his concern. They had still descended from Walter, the sixth steward to the throne, who'd married the daughter of Robert the Bruce. Now a Prussian Hanoverian ruled over Scotland and that was a concern, but he held his peace. For now.

He gestured to Thea. "Please continue."

"Where was I? Oh, yes," Thea said. "So, Zeus proclaimed that each of them—Athena and Poseidon— would give a gift to Cecrops and he would decide which to choose. Poseidon took his trident and struck a rock and an eternal spring gushed forth." Thea touched the three-pronged forklike spear on the statue. "But being god of the sea, he'd made the water salty, and the people were not able to drink from it." She moved to the other figurine. "Athena, on the other hand, planted a seed which grew into an olive tree that provided both food and oil for lamps for the people."

"And Ceclops chose Athena's gift," Moire said, "and that's why the city is called Athens."

"Exactly."

Moire snickered. "I think it shows women are smarter than men."

"Debatable," Ian muttered.

"I'm sure the subject is," Thea said soothingly, although he could tell she was trying not to smile at

Moire's remark. "However, there is a different outcome to think about here."

"Which is?" he asked, only slightly mollified that she hadn't laughed out loud.

"Offering an olive branch," she promptly responded, "which is what Athena gave her uncle as a gift to ensure there were no hard feelings."

She paused and waited for him to say something. Since he was pretty sure he knew where she was leading with this, he kept quiet. She sighed.

"You aren't going to ask what the moral of the story is, are you?"

"I doona think—"

"Well, I will," Moire said. "What is it?"

"That sometimes," Thea answered, "discussing strategies can lead to a solution with less bloodshed." She turned to look at Ian directly. "Sometimes, war can even be avoided."

"'Tis too late—"

"Ian!" Ardsheal stood in the doorway. "Word's just arrived Cromartie is returning to Stirling, empty-handed."

****

Thea said a silent prayer of thanks when Moire insisted they stay to hear what the messenger had to say. Ardsheal hadn't been too pleased, but she'd reminded him she was Cromartie's niece and had a right to know what was happening. Thea moved unobtrusively to a chair tucked into a corner of the room and hoped no one would notice her. She breathed a sigh of relief when the messenger walked in and no one asked her to leave.

"The prince sent Cromartie south to recruit more troops," Ardsheal said when the man was seated. "What happened?"

"The report said the general wasn't having much success in gaining northern border support."

Ardsheal raised his brows. "Even though they've been neglected by the English king in the region?"

The man shrugged. "They wanted to stay neutral."

"Cowards," Ian muttered. "A man needs to take a stance and not sit on the fence waiting to see which side wins."

Thea chewed her lip. It made sense to her that northern England would hesitate to take a side, even if they weren't necessarily in favor of King George. Derby wasn't in Scotland, after all. Avoiding bloodshed was wise, not cowardly, in her estimation, but it seemed it wasn't in Ian's view.

"Aye, but there was another reason," the messenger said. "The French boats that were supposed to dock on the River Derwent didn't arrive and, since the general's men had left heavy artillery behind so they could move more swiftly, they were without logistical support, which left them vulnerable."

Thea bit her tongue to keep quiet. The French ships wouldn't be arriving, even though King Louis had signed an agreement with Prince Charles's father, the "Old Pretender," after the victory of Prestopans to support the effort to return a Stuart to the throne. The attempt to make the passage had been met by a British blockade, thanks in part to a previous, unrelated attempt by the French to invade England. Besides which, Thea felt pretty sure King Louis' attention was on protecting France's interests in the war of Austrian Succession that was currently happening on the Continent. But her thoughts were wandering.

"Ye think the people of Derby might have turned on us if the general hadn't retreated?" Ardsheal asked.

"'Twas nae clear, but the possibility was there."

"Cromartie wouldna put that in a missive anyway," Ian said.

"True," Ardsheal agreed. "At least, his regiment can now join the prince."

The messenger nodded. "There's already talk of that. Since the English are on the march toward Stirling, Cromartie has requested you bring men and meet him at Stirling. The prince and General Murray are going to launch a surprise attack at Falkirk."

Ian's head whipped around so fast that Thea was afraid she'd hear a crack in his neck. His wolf-colored eyes were penetrating as he stared at her. She held his gaze and gave an almost imperceptible nod.

What the messenger had said confirmed the prediction she'd given Ian earlier. But was it enough for him to believe she was from the future?

Chapter Six

The request for his cousin to travel to Stirling had the entire castle in a state of upheaval. Not only did the men who had been training need to sharpen their swords, dirks and other weapons, but provisions needed to be packed for the nearly week-long march south. A hundred men on the march could hardly stay at inns, although they could likely lodge in crofter's barns and outbuildings at night. But farmers and tenants could hardly be expected to provide food for that number. While his cousin was issuing orders to ready the men, Mrs. Moffett was acting like an efficient general, giving instructions to various maids, cooks, and ghillies who were shuttling back and forth, arms laden with supplies.

But the uproar that was going on inside and outside the castle wasn't what was bothering Ian. He was in a mental uproar with himself,

How could Thea Ross have known about Falkirk? She had said his cousin should be taking part in that battle and now, apparently, he would be. How had she known that?

His mind refused to accept the explanation she had given. It simply wasn't possible that she was from the future. He'd be barmy if he accepted it. Then again, if he kept trying to figure it out, he might go barmy anyway.

Looking around at the somewhat organized chaos, he wondered where she was. He spotted Cora heading toward the kitchens. She smiled when he beckoned her over.

"Aye?" She tilted her head. "Ye look a wee bit frazzled."

He was not frazzled. Or, maybe he was. He wasn't sure anymore.

Cora's smile widened as she reached up and stroked the side of his face with her hand. "What can I do for ye, Ian?"

He took a step back, not wanting to encourage her flirtation. When he'd first arrived at the Black Isle, he'd thought Cora was simply friendly, but she had begun acting overly familiar in recent weeks. "Have ye seen Miss Ross?"

Her smile faded. "Why?"

Ian tried not to frown. Cora had a tendency to be impertinent—probably because she was the surgeon's daughter and he wielded a certain amount of authority. Ian usually tended to overlook her remarks. "I need to talk to Miss Ross."

Her lower lip stuck out in a pout. "She was bothering my father, the last I saw."

This time he did frown. "Bothering your father?"

"Aye. She was telling him what to do."

"Telling him what to do?" Ian felt like a parrot. "Why would she be doing that? What are ye talking about?"

"She was trying to tell him what medical supplies he needed to put in the wagons." Cora's chin jutted out. "She has nae business acting like she kens more than my father."

Ian suppressed a curse. He didn't need Thea offering her "future knowledge"—whatever it might be—to

Callum Chattan, who'd had just enough training that he thought himself an expert on nearly every aspect of medicine, which he definitely also thought was strictly a man's field.

Ian turned away. He'd best get to the surgery before real blood was spilled.

****

"Of course I know what I'm talking about." Thea had the childish urge to stamp her foot in frustration. She'd known chauvinistic men in her century, but Callum Chattan made them all seem like chivalrous knights instead. Maybe her first clue should have been when he'd glared at her while asking what she was doing in his surgery when she'd come through the door. But she always tried to give people the benefit of the doubt. The man was hectically trying to decide if any soldiers weren't fit for travel after all. That's when she'd offered to do basic TPR—temperature, pulse, respiration—on the men waiting to be checked. You'd think she'd asked to assist him in removing a limb. That a number of the soldiers had grinned and moved over to form a line beside her probably hadn't helped. She sighed. The place had cleared out. Maybe now he'd listen.

"I'm only offering what I've learned about the healing arts myself."

"I doona need your help."

Thea smiled pleasantly, although she felt her teeth grinding. "My late husband was studying to be a doctor of osteopathy—"

"Of what? Never heard of it."

She managed to keep her smile in place. "Osteopathy relies on manipulation of the body and natural remedies—"

"Doona sound natural to me."

She stopped smiling. "Would you let me explain?"

"Doona need explaining. Just leave—"

"Now, Callum. Have ye forgotten your manners?" Ian stood in the doorway, frowning slightly.

Callum frowned back. "The Sassenach is interfering—"

"Miss Ross is from Nova Scotia," Ian said, "and, in case ye didna hear me, her last name is Ross."

"I heard ye," Callum mumbled. "She's still interfering."

Ian looked around. "With what, exactly?"

"I was trying to convince Mr. Chattan that he should pack some herbal supplies for the soldiers," Thea said. "Things like witch hazel and hemlock for poultices to stop bleeding, sphagnum moss for wounds, juniper as an astringent—"

"A what?" Ian asked.

"An astringent…it helps keep germs out of cuts and prevents infection."

"Ye see what I mean?" Callum asked. "The woman is talking nonsense."

"I am not! It's well known…" Thea stopped at the confused expression on Ian's face that swiftly changed to consternation. She realized then that germs had not yet been "discovered" nor recognized as the cause for infection. It wouldn't help her case if she said it was common knowledge in her century, nor would it help if she said she'd read about it in medical books. "This is what I was told by someone very wise," she finished rather lamely.

Callum gave her a suspicious look. "Like that old hag Maggie in the woods, practicing her witchcraft, nae doubt."

"There are nae witches," Ian said sharply. "Ye ken that, Callum."

"Well, the old hag ran off. Why would she do that if she werena afraid of burning?"

The woman sounded smart to her. If Maggie'd been a *real* witch, she could have uttered a curse to stop them. Thea managed not to say it.

Ian ignored Callum's comment and turned to Thea. "I need ye to come with me to the house."

She nodded, wondering if she was in for a real scold once they were out of earshot. She didn't really care, if it was an opportunity to escape in a somewhat dignified manner.

The man snorted as they left. "Just because we doona burn them anymore doesna mean they are nae out there."

****

Having delivered Thea into Moire's somewhat dubious custody—she had a penchant for getting into trouble too—Ian joined Ardsheal in the study.

"Ye think ye'll be ready to leave in the morn?" he asked.

"We'll have to be ready," his cousin replied. "'Tis at least a week's march from here and Hawley's already got a head start on us heading toward Stirling. Supposedly he's travelling with seven thousand troops, so every regiment the prince can add will help."

"Hopefully, he willna ken that the prince has been alerted."

Ardsheal gave him a rueful look. "That many men on the road would be hard to miss, but I'll wager Hawley is too arrogant to care. His orders are—as best we know—to take over command at Stirling. He'll be prepared to fight his way through a blockade."

"He'll be expecting that to happen at the castle and nae be expecting an intercept at Falkirk." According to Thea, this would happen on Janaury seventeenth, but Ian wasn't about to say that lest his cousin think he'd gone touched in the head. Which was a distinct possibility since he was even considering that Thea might know something.

"Aye. That seems to be the plan." His cousin pushed a stack of papers across the desk to him. "I'm sorry to be leaving ye with all of this, since I ken ye hate the paperwork, but since ye'll now be in command of Kilcoy, ye'll need to keep up with it. Cromartie would have the same faith in ye as he did in me."

Another good reason not to mention a specific date for the battle. His cousin was entrusting him not only to continue to train recruits as they came in, but also to handle the details of running an estate in the absence of the earl. If Ardsheal thought he had taken to listening to predictions of the future, he'd be hesitant to turn everything over.

Then, too, there was the problem with Callum, although Ian wasn't about to burden his cousin with what had just transpired in the surgery. If wounded men from Falkirk were sent north to recover, the surgeon would have his hands full. Thea—he was already beginning to recognize a willful streak in her—would insist on helping the man who didn't want her help. Ian hadn't liked Callum's references to witches, either. Even though Scotland had banned witch hunts and the last "burning" had taken place nineteen years ago at Dornach, superstition still remained. Any woman who seemed "different" could be at risk of being singled out, with dire consequences.

Thea could definitely be considered "different." And now, given command of Kilcoy, it was his duty and responsibility to make sure that didn't happen.

****

Thea wedged herself into a corner behind a column of the portico that ran along part of the back side of the castle. From this vantage point she could watch the goings-on in the courtyard unobserved. More specifically, she could watch Ian unobserved as he practiced fencing with the new recruits that John Ross had sent earlier in the week. Thankfully, her "kin" had not accompanied the group, so she wouldn't have to answer questions or make up stories.

They were experiencing a January thaw, and Ian had removed both vest and shirt as he took on one recruit after another, testing their skills and agility. There was no question about his skill or agility. Sweat glistened off his broad chest as his shoulders and biceps bulged and contracted with various swipes of his sword. His muscular legs, encased in tight-fitting leather breeches, rippled smoothly as he lunged, and his footwork would have put to shame any of those professional dancers on that TV show that was so popular.

Thea had accidently stumbled across the men practicing several days ago while on her way back from fetching eggs at the henhouse. She'd almost dropped the basket she carried at the sight of Ian looking like some medieval warrior, his dark hair flying behind him as he sidestepped, spun and whirled, sword flashing in the sun. After delivering the eggs—unbroken—to Cook, she'd slipped back outside and found this secluded spot in which to hide. She'd taken to doing daily trips to the henhouse as an excuse ever since.

Since Ardsheal had left nearly ten days ago, she hadn't had much of a chance to talk with Ian. He'd spent the first few days secluded in the study, going over accounts and other dealings with the estate. She'd seen him mainly at the evening meals, which Cora and her father also attended. Ian kept the conversation general. She didn't know if it was because he was afraid she'd bring up the future or if it was because he didn't want Callum launching another verbal attack. Or maybe it was because of Cora. The girl made it quite obvious she was enamored of Ian. Not that Thea could blame her, since she was beginning to feel somewhat enamored herself, which was really stupid, given her circumstances. Still, here she was, peeking out from her hiding place to watch him.

Something moved in her peripheral vision and she turned her head and squinted down the shaded row of pillars. In the opposite corner at the far end stood Cora. Only she wasn't watching Ian at the moment. Cora was watching her.

A chill stole over Thea that had nothing to do with temperature.

Chapter Seven

Ian wasn't particularly surprised when Thea knocked on the study door and stuck her head around it. The messenger that Ardsheal sent from Stirling had just left.

"May I come in?"

He stood. "Of course."

As she entered, she gave him a cautious look. "You don't seem surprised to see me."

"I was rather expecting ye." He gave her a wry smile as he gestured for her to sit. "What surprises me is that ye didna ask to sit in on the conference."

Thea shook her head as she took a seat near the hearth. "I wanted you to hear the facts first hand from someone who was actually at Falkirk. Now, we'll see if I was right."

She'd already been right about the date, which was eerie enough. Ian still hadn't figured out how she could have known that. She'd been right about the general outcome as well, although the latter could have been an educated guess. There was always a fifty-percent chance of one side winning. There wasn't any way she could know the details of what happened at the battle, so it would be interesting to see how her account lined up with the messenger's. He took the chair opposite hers.

"Go on, then."

"All right. First, the battle was fought near dusk with

heavy snow falling, right?"

Ian nodded. That was something anyone could figure out, given that they'd had a near blizzard at Inverness.

"Hawley was surprised and he led off with his cavalry, didn't he?"

"That's often the case with the English, lass."

"Except in this case, the ground was already muddy, given the thaw earlier this month, and the horses churned it up, making it harder for the infantry to follow."

"That's logical enough."

Thea chewed her lip and Ian was momentarily distracted. She had no way of knowing how enticing that little movement was.

"I believe your cousin was fighting alongside General Murray, attacking Hawley's right wing, which was holding firm. Hawley's left wing was routed, but the general didn't know it because Lt. General Drummond arrived late and hadn't had time to confer with General Murray."

Ian's attention snapped back. "How did ye ken that? Were ye listening at the door?"

She scowled at him. "I was not. You can ask Moire, if you don't believe me. We were both in the kitchen."

He frowned too. "Then how did ye ken it?"

"Because…" She let out a long sigh. "…I really am from the future." Thea held up a hand before he could protest. "Let me finish. The Jacobites didn't know the left wing had been broken, so they retreated to Stirling thinking they'd lost. The right wing, realizing the left was fleeing and leaving cannon and artillery behind, fled with them, thinking they'd lost too. Total confusion, although really a Jacobite victory." She folded her hands in her lap. "Am I right?"

Ian was stunned. Thea's narrative had followed Ardsheal's messenger's almost perfectly. There had been a dispute over responsibility between Murray and Drummond with each claiming the other was the one who didn't follow through. Murray blamed Drummond for being late and Drummond blamed Murray for letting his men sack the English camp instead of pursuing the Redcoats.

"Am I right?" Thea asked again.

Ian slowly nodded. "I doona ken how ye got all the facts, but aye, ye are right. 'Tis how it happened."

Thea opened her mouth, then closed it and shook her head "You still don't believe me, do you?"

He raised a brow. "That ye are from the future? Nae, I doona believe it. 'Tis impossible."

"You keep saying that." She sighed again. "I won't argue with you anymore."

"Good. Then that's over and done."

"No, it isn't." She rose and walked to the door, then turned to him. "What I am going to do is keep predicting what will happen. Eventually, you'll have to believe me."

Ian stared at the open door after she left. Thea seemed to be quite sane in all other aspects of her actions and conversations, except for this notion that she was from another century. He really wished John Ross had brought the new recruits himself so he could have talked with him.

Someone had to know who Thea Ross really was.

****

Thea meant what she said. She was going to keep on predicting events leading up to Culloden. Thankfully, her friend Vi had been—or would be—a history professor and had regaled both Charlotte and herself with dates, names, and places ad nauseam prior to their trip to Scotland—in the twenty-first century—so she knew what was going to happen.

Still, she had to be careful lest Ian actually think she was not sane. After their talk yesterday, she's seen him talking to the messenger as the man was leaving. With his frequent glances back toward the upstairs bedroom that she occupied, she suspected he was trying to verify more facts. Even now, as they were seated at the dinner table, he kept glancing at her as he filled Callum in about Falkirk. She was pretty sure those glances were warnings not to contribute to the conversation. Given that he was speaking to Callum, she decided it best to refrain.

"So when are ye planning to go back to Nova Scotia?" Cora asked once the discussion had subsided.

Thea blinked at the abruptness of the question. "I hadn't really thought about it."

Ian frowned. "Miss Ross may stay as long as she wishes."

"Thank you," Thea replied and turned back to Cora, forcing a smile. "I lack funds at this point anyway."

Cora didn't return the smile. "Ye are a Ross. Your kin could help ye."

"Did I nae just say Miss Ross can stay for as long as she likes?" Ian asked. His voice was calm, but his eyes glittered like shards of glass.

Cora adopted a mulish look. "I just thought she'd like to go back to her family."

"Aye. 'Tis always best to be with kin," her father said as he looked at Thea. "What part of Nova Scotia are ye from again?"

Thea hesitated. She'd mentioned her parents had a summer home in Halifax to Ian and he hadn't questioned that, probably because he was flummoxed by the whole idea of her being from the future, but Halifax wouldn't be founded until three years from now, in 1749. "I'm from Cape Breton Island." Thankfully, that territory had been discovered as early as 1497 when John Cabot landed on its shores.

"Sounds French to me."

"Originally, it was. The French were some of the first European settlers, establishing Port Royal in 1605 and then the fortress at Louisbourg in 1713."

Thea felt somewhat amazed that she was actually recalling Vi's history lectures so well. If Callum Chattan wanted to know her background, he was going to get it.

"But then," she continued, "England started fighting the French for the territory, rather like what's going on right now on the Continent." The Canadian conflict would actually last well over a hundred years, but that was information she'd best keep to herself. "Eventually, British people started settling over there." She shrugged. "My grandparents were some of the Scots that went over." That wasn't a lie. It just hadn't happened in this century.

Callum narrowed his eyes at her. "I never heard of any Ross moving across the sea."

Thea managed to smile pleasantly at the man, although she was longing to throw something at him. "My grandfather was a MacDonald." She didn't add that in a few short years, there would be thousands of MacDonalds going over. For that matter, Vi had said that in the twenty-first century there were almost as many Canadians with Scottish heritage as there would be Scots in Scotland. Thea sighed inwardly. Definitely not information she could share.

"MacDonalds." Callum snorted. "Always seeking new land. Nae satisfied with controlling most of the Isles."

"Well..." Thea forced a smile again. "Their ancestors were Norsemen, after all."

"And doona forget," Ian said, "that Alexander MacDonald, laird of Keppoch, was one of the first to support the prince once he landed on our shores."

"Did he nae support the prince's father in the 1715 uprising too?" Moire asked.

"Aye," Ian replied. "The MacDonalds have always been on Scotland's side."

"Most likely because of Glencoe." Callum gave Thea a direct look. "At least he didna hie off to foreign parts to be safe."

"That would be cowardly, nae?" Cora asked, her eyes innocently wide.

Thea sighed inwardly. She wasn't going to win this argument, although she wasn't even sure why it was an argument.

"I think advertising for cheap land was the reason a lot of Scots left their homeland," Ian said. "'Tis nae a crime—or cowardly—to want a better life for a man's family."

Since both Cora and her father looked like they wanted to argue further, Thea decided to try changing the subject. "Since there are a lot of towns named after Scottish ones, I'm sure the immigrants missed their native land." She managed another smile. "Did you know there is an Inverness in Nova Scotia?" It wouldn't be established until 1904, but that was probably not relevant. "They even refer to the farthest northerly point as the Cape Breton Highlands…and Dingwall—just like the town near here—is at the very end." It was actually an unincorporated area that was established in the 1800s, but Thea's objective was to draw a—hopefully—comforting comparison.

"I dinna ken that! 'Tis interesting that our kinsmen have nae forgotten us." Moire turned to Cora. "Do ye nae think so?"

"I suppose so," the girl mumbled.

Ian gave Thea a thoughtful look, but she was thankful the conversation drifted back to talk about the victory at Falkirk. Thea finished the rest of her meal in silence, excusing herself quickly when they'd finished. She suspected Ian wanted to question her more about Nova Scotia, and she needed time to think about its history. It might be helpful in convincing him to accept the truth. Then again, it might just convince him she was truly brain-addled. She needed time to think.

****

Cora watched Thea go. Ever since that bitch had come to Kilcoy, Ian had been protective of her and short with Cora. He rebuffed her and she didn't like it. She didn't like it at all. She wanted to marry Ian and her father had no objections. Ian was very braw and very handsome, and she was more than willing to lift her skirts for him, although as her father told her, she'd have to make sure they were caught when she did.

Now Ian had no time for her. It was like he was under a spell. Cora frowned, remembering the conversation she'd overheard. The woman spoke strangely. She was also unusual-looking with her pale hair and silvery eyes. Could she be a witch?

Chapter Eight

"What do the two of ye think you're doing?" Ian blocked the entrance to the stables several days later as Moire and Thea led two mares forward.

Moire's expression told him he was daft. "I would say it looks like we're going for a ride."

"I can see that—"

"Then why do ye ask? I'm planning to show Thea the Moray Firth."

He frowned. "Without an escort?"

She rolled her eyes. "In case ye have nae noticed, Ardsheal took my usual escort with him. The stable boys are busy."

"Ye ken full well ye are nae to ride out alone."

She smirked. "I have Thea with me."

"She hardly qualifies as an escort." He looked at Thea and was immediately distracted. She was wearing one of Moire's riding habits and, since she was taller, the divided skirt didn't quite meet the half-boots she wore, exposing a bit of leg, and the jacket hugged her frame, outlining generous breasts. She'd left several buttons open of the white shirt she wore and Ian caught a glimpse of cleavage. Her skin looked like creamy satin, and for a moment he envisioned himself stroking it with his fingers.

A loud clearing of Moire's throat snapped him out of his fantasy.

"Are ye going to move?" Moire tapped her foot.

He folded his arms across his chest. "Nae."

Moire turned to Thea. "I told ye I was a hostage."

"Ye are nae a hostage," he all but growled.

"Then why can't we go for a ride?" Thea asked. "I'd like to explore a bit to see if the countryside looks like the Highlands in Nova Scotia. I've been told it does."

Ian drew his brows together, about to ask who had told her that, but thought better of it. He didn't want her saying something about someone from the future telling her.

"How high are your mountains?" Moire asked.

"The highest is White Hill, which is about seventeen hundred feet," Thea replied. 'How high are yours?"

"Our munros are the highest, over three thousand."

"But ye willna find those on the Black Isle," Ian said. "They're a ways westerly of us."

Thea smiled. "We don't need to ride that far. I'd just like to see the countryside." The mare suddenly tossed her head, jerking the reins away from Thea. Ian grabbed them before the animal could barrel past him.

"Sorry. I let the reins go slack." Thea held out her hand. "I'll take those back."

He held on to them and gave Thea a dubious look. "Are ye sure ye ken how to ride?"

She bristled. "Of course I do. I grew up on a ranch in Tex—"

"Nova Scotia has ranches?" Ian quickly interrupted. The lass was going to say Texas, he was sure of it. And he was also sure there was no Texas. For her own protection, she shouldn't be talking like that in front of Moire.

"What's a ranch?"

Ian groaned inwardly at Moire's question. He should have known she wouldn't let a statement like that go. He just hoped Thea's answer would be rational—and believable.

"It's like a very large farm." Thea glanced at him before turning back to Moire. "Kind of like the estate here at Kilcoy, but without a castle." She glanced at Ian again. "Nova Scotia has no need of castles."

He breathed a sigh of relief. At least she hadn't mentioned Texas.

"And where is Tex?" Moire asked.

So much for feeling relieved. "Is it nae a part of Nova Scotia, lass?"

Thea gave him an unwavering stare and he was afraid she was going to argue the point, but then she nodded. "It is farther south than where my parents live."

Moire's horse stamped a hoof and she patted the mare's neck. "Are ye going to let us ride or nae?"

He wasn't about to let the two of them go off without an escort, and he didn't trust the new recruits enough yet to assign one of them. But, if he kept Moire and Thea here, they'd no doubt go off together and who knows what questions Moire would ask or how Thea would answer them. Ian sighed. "Let me saddle my horse and I'll go with ye."

****

As they set off following a path no wider than a deer trail that wound around tree roots and jutting rocks, Thea was glad Highlanders were practical, particularly in the women wearing a divided skirt that allowed her to ride astride. She could only imagine how uncomfortable it would be to sit sidesaddle over this type of ground. She doubted the horse would have appreciated the uneven weight distribution, either. And it did feel good to be outside, riding in the countryside.

Ian rode a horse like he did everything else…very well. Thea's mare, a rather placid animal that Thea wouldn't have chosen, although she understood it was a cautious choice for a rider whose expertise was not known, was content to follow behind, which gave her the unexpected benefit of watching Ian unobserved.

Since she'd grown up on a ranch in Texas—regardless that Ian put the location in Nova Scotia—she'd had plenty of experience in riding and watching cowboys do real work with their horses. While they were obviously adept, every once in a while she'd spot a rider who actually seemed to effortlessly be a part of the horse and they'd move as one entity. Ian was one of those. Although they had not yet cantered, there was no jostling or bouncing on the trot, his muscular thighs simply clung to the gelding's flanks. And earlier, as they were leaving, when his mount had spooked and reared at a hare darting across the path, he'd barely shifted in the saddle as he brought the animal under control. That had riveted her attention on how well he sat his horse. And he had light hands…the gelding's mouth was not pulled and the reins were not taut. Thea found herself wondering how gentle Ian's hands would be caressing her. Stroking along her ribs, close to her… She shook her head to clear that silly fantasy, wherever it had come from.

"Is something wrong?"

Ian halted at Moire's question and looked back at her. "Are ye having trouble with the mare?"

"No." The only trouble she was having was lapsing off into fantasyland. Thinking about Ian's muscular thighs, nice arse, and powerfully gentle hands—

goodness, she'd never thought about parts of Alan's anatomy—wasn't going to help her convince Ian to believe they could prevent the outcome of Culloden if he'd just listen to her.

"Then why were ye shaking your head?" Moire asked.

'I…uh…I guess I was just doing that out of amazement for the scenery. It's so beautiful out here. It reminds me of Nova Scotia." It sounded a little bit lame, since they'd been following a rocky trail on relatively flat land, heading toward the firth for a good half hour.

Ian raised a brow. "I thought ye said the place was mountainous?"

Was he suspecting her of making up the place? Thea sighed inwardly. He probably was, since he didn't believe she was from the future. But regardless of which century she was in, the landscape in Canada hadn't really changed.

"The northern peninsula is mountainous, very much like your Highlands. That's why the Scots who migrated call it that," she added for emphasis. "But farther south, on the eastern coast, it is very much like this…a rocky shoreline. In fact," she said, hoping to switch the subject, "I think I can hear the waves. We must be close?"

"Aye." Ian gave her a scrutinizing look before glancing at her horse. "Are ye sure ye can handle the mare? The water is a bit rough this time of year. With the tide coming in, there's nae much of a beach."

"I rode horses back home." She really wanted to tell him that, in Texas, she'd ridden Quarter horses known for their ability for quick starts and sharp turns. She'd even done her share of helping her father's ranch hands herd cattle, but explaining that would probably cement the notion in Ian's head that she was touched in hers.

"I'll be fine." She patted the mare's neck. "I have a feeling she'll be fine too."

He looked doubtful and, for a moment, she wondered if he was going to take the reins and actually lead her along or…maybe he would act like a hero from one of Charlotte's novels and pull her across his saddle to nestle in front of him…? She blinked rapidly. What in the world was coming over her? Her mind never ran off in those directions. Thea managed to smile at him. "Perhaps we should move along before the tide is fully in and we get in trouble?"

"That's a good idea," Moire said and nudged her horse forward.

Ian made a sound that resembled a growl as he turned his horse too. "We willna stay long since I doona want to put us in danger."

As Thea's mare followed him, she thought there was more than one kind of danger and she was perilously close to becoming a victim.

****

Ian closed the ledger and shoved it aside, then leaned back in the chair behind the desk in the study. The numbers appeared to be in order, although he couldn't be sure, given that he was having trouble concentrating.

Thea was becoming more and more of a dilemma. He had spent the last few days since their ride going over her remarks in his mind. She seemed obsessed with this place called Texas. Cromartie had an excellent set of maps that included Nova Scotia and the colonies. He'd spread them out, gone over them inch by inch, but couldn't find any place called Texas. He was at his wit's end, trying to figure the lass.

He'd been surprised at her detailed description of Nova Scotia since he thought it was only part of the story they'd created to explain her appearance, but then he remembered that she was the one who'd come up with the idea of her parents living there. Maybe they actually did. Maybe she had too and maybe even the part of her husband being killed was true. She'd said she was a widow, and he hadn't asked how it had happened. Still. Even if all those things were true, it didn't explain why she'd suddenly shown up at Hogmanay nor how she'd gotten there, without an escort or any money or worldly goods. And it didn't explain Texas.

He closed his eyes and rubbed his temples, willing the headache that was beginning to form to go away. He didn't think Thea was mind-addled, but what other explanation could there be? She couldn't be from the future. She…

"May I come in?"

Startled, he opened his eyes to find Thea standing in the doorway. For a moment, he thought maybe he'd conjured her, which made him wonder if he wasn't the one who was addle-brained.

"Of course." He started to rise, but she waved him to stay seated while she took the chair in front of the desk. "What is it?"

As she chewed her lip, it turned red and swelled, which made him want to cover that luscious mouth with his. He pushed his lustful thoughts aside. Thea chewed her lip when she was nervous, not passionate.

"Is something wrong?"

"Not exactly."

Her tongue darted out to lick her wet lips and Ian shifted in his chair as his groin stirred. He was grateful he was sitting behind the desk.

"What is it then?"

"A rider just arrived—"

"A messenger? From Cromartie or the prince?"

"I don't think so."

"Then from where? Ye are nae making sense, lass."

Thea paused. "I think he's coming from Edinburgh."

Ian frowned. "Is it about Hawley then? That he's regrouping?"

"I don't think so," she said again and took a deep breath. "I think what he's going to tell you is that the Duke of Cumberland has arrived there."

"Cumberland? The king recalled him from Flanders to protect London from a French invasion," Ian said. "Why would he come north?"

"The French invasion isn't going to happen," Thea replied, "and Hawley has been disgraced. King George will be replacing him with his son, the duke."

"Did ye already talk to the man?"

Thea gave him a direct look. "Not yet."

"Then how…" He stopped and shook his head. "Doona tell me ye are predicting the future again."

She winced a little, but didn't look away. "I'm telling you what is going to happen."

"Ye canna ken…" He paused at the sound of a shuffle in the hall and looked toward the door. "Who's there?"

"'Tis just me." Cora appeared in the doorway. Her gaze narrowed on Thea before she turned back to Ian. "I was sent to tell ye there's a messenger from Edinburgh to see ye."

For a moment, Ian felt lightheaded. How had Thea known? As the blood rushed back to his brain, another

thought occurred, even more dangerous.
How much had Cora heard?

Chapter Nine

A week later, Thea stood outside the study door, hesitating. She needed to ask a favor of Ian, and when she did, he would want to know why, and when she told him, he wouldn't like the answer. It had to be done, though. It was only a matter of days before wounded soldiers would be arriving. She knocked.

"Enter."

As she opened the door and stepped inside, Ian looked up from a stack of paperwork and smiled. "Come in and sit. Ye are a welcome intrusion from all of this."

He probably wouldn't think so once she told him why she was here. Still, a bit of pleasant, prior conversation might be advisable. "What are you working on?"

"Estate matters."

"Like what?"

"Mostly mundane matters. I doona want to bore ye."

"You won't bore me. Maybe I can help… I've run a household before."

He gave her a dubious look, even though she hadn't said she'd run a future household. Didn't women take charge of that in this century?

"Mrs. Moffett takes care of that, so I doona ken what ye could do. This…" He gestured to the stack of papers. "…has to do with running the estate. With Elliott gone, I've got to tally the amount we need to compensate the tradesmen. I also need to inventory what we receive from the crofters and insure there's enough barley seed for the spring planting or we won't have any harvest for whisky in the fall."

Thea pulled her bottom lip between her teeth. Distilling whisky was the least of the upcoming problems. Spring planting might not happen at all this year if the battle at Culloden took place. Besides the senseless massacre, the Scots would have most of their basic rights taken away by the English.

"I'm wondering…" She paused. "…since the prince has never lived in Scotland, has anyone talked to him about the importance of the people being left in peace to attend to crofting, crops, and distilling whisky?"

He gave her a puzzled look. "I doona ken what conversations the prince has had, but I doona ken what a difference it would make."

"Well, war interferes with all that." Thea tried not to sound annoyed. "To say nothing of destruction and senseless killing."

"We doona have a choice, lass. Scotland needs its rightful king—a Stuart—on the throne, not some Prussian imposter."

"I understand you don't want to be under English rule, but the king is not exactly an imposter."

Ian frowned. "He's nae a Stuart."

This was where studying the Stuart lineage began to cloud. "True, but when both Queen Mary and Queen Anne died without heirs, the throne passed to the Hanovers."

His frown deepened. "Who are nae Stuarts."

"That's probably true—"

"It is true."

"Yes," she said in order to pacify him, "but the Act of Settlement, rightly or wrongly—"

"Wrongly." Ian folded his arms across his chest.

Thea tried not to notice how powerful those arms were or how broad his chest. Was he trying to distract her? Probably not, given the glare in his eyes. She sighed. "Wrongly then, but it legally kept a Catholic from ascending the throne, which is why James Francis Edward Stuart—the prince's father—was overlooked and the crown went to Electress Sophia of Hanover, who was a sister of Charles I."

"I seem to remember that Charles I lost his head," Ian said. "Literally."

"Yes, well. Sophia was also the cousin of James VII and granddaughter of James VI." She gave him a questioning look. "Isn't that enough Stuart relationships?"

Ian straightened, which made his biceps bulge and his shoulders look even wider. Thea narrowed her eyes. Maybe he was trying to distract her.

"Electress Sophia didna become queen."

So much for distraction. Thea sighed again. "George I was her son—"

"—who spent little time in England, let alone Scotland."

"But his son—the current king—is very much English."

Ian smiled. "I think ye just lost your arguments, lass. George II is definitely English." His smile widened. "Which is why we want a Scottish king…a Stuart." He flexed his arms and lowered them.

He really was trying to distract her, she was sure of it. She smiled too, although it felt forced. She wanted to say that Charles Edward Stuart—their Bonnie Prince Charlie—wasn't actually from Scotland either, but she managed to hold her tongue. "What I am trying to say is that maybe a war can be avoided if some kind of compromise can be made."

Ian snorted. "A good compromise would be for old George to leave Britain altogether."

Thea looked heavenward. "That's not a compromise."

'Hmph. The Prussian imposter could surrender Scotland to us, then." Ian lifted a shoulder—a very broad shoulder—in a semi-shrug. "We Scots are nae greedy. We only want what is rightfully ours…and that is to be ruled by a Stuart king."

"Who wasn't born in Scotland." There. She'd said it.

He drew his brows together. "He would have been if his grandfather James hadn't been forced into exile by William of Orange." Ian muttered something under his breath that was most likely a curse. "And we also ken the bloody Dutchman was responsible for the massacre of MacDonalds at Glen Coe."

"And there will be another bloody massacre if this war isn't stopped." Thea's temper flared, which was rare. "A battle at Culloden will shed real blood."

Ian deepened his frown. "Are ye talking about Drummossie Moor? Why would there be a battle there?"

Thea chewed her lip again. She hadn't meant to talk about that battle quite yet—there were so many things to precede it—but maybe it was just as well that she come out with it. "Because Cumberland will eventually move his army to Aberdeen and then march toward Inverness this spring. Your prince will insist on meeting his advance. They'll meet at Culloden and…" She paused. "…the Scots will lose."

Ian stared at her. For a long moment he was silent. Thea was beginning to think maybe she had pushed him too far. She might very well find herself locked in an attic—or a dungeon, if Kilcoy had one—in a very short time. Still. She raised her chin defiantly and stared back. He had to know what was going to happen.

He finally sighed. "I suppose ye ken this because ye are from the future."

It wasn't a question. He didn't sound sarcastic, only resigned. He obviously didn't believe her. She sighed too. "It's the truth. Unless circumstances change, nearly fifteen hundred Scots will die on April 16th."

Ian studied her for another long moment before he shook his head. "Ye have got to stop talking like this, ere someone thinks ye mad."

Like you? She wanted to ask, but her rational mind was beginning to take over. She would have the same reaction if the situation were reversed. She just needed to predict smaller things to convince him, which reminded her why she had come in to the study in the first place. She sighed again. So much for small talk. This conversation wasn't going to make her asking for a favor any easier.

"I can't blame you for not believing me, but I didn't stop in to argue with you…about the Stuart kings or the future."

"Hmmm. Why did ye come in?"

"I need for you to take me into Inverness."

Ian raised a brow. "Ye doona want to reenact the scene by the castle again, do ye?"

"No. There's no portal… I mean, there's nothing

there."

"At least ye agree about that." He tilted his head. "So what do ye need in Inverness?"

"Supplies. Medical supplies," she added when he gave her a questioning look.

"Callum takes care of those."

"Well, yes, but…" Callum didn't know that germs caused infections and certain herbs could heal them. He didn't know about antiseptics like vinegar that could prevent wounds from festering. She had to choose her words carefully though, since it was probably better she didn't talk about modern medicine right now. "The Scots that migrated to Nova Scotia learned about medicines that the native Mi'Kmaq people used. I thought I might pick up some of those items at the apothecary."

"I doona think Callum would use them."

"He wouldn't have to. I would."

Both of Ian's brows rose. "I doona think Callum would welcome that either."

"Probably not." Thea wouldn't argue that point. "But I know some of those…medicines…can save lives."

He hesitated, then nodded. "All right. I'll think on it."

"How long will you think on it?"

'I doona ken." He shrugged. "There's nae rush since we have nae wounded."

"But you will." Thea could have bitten her tongue. That wasn't supposed to come out. Not now.

A brow lifted again. "Do ye have another prediction of the future?"

Was he teasing her? Thea's temper began to rise again, a very unusual thing to happen twice in so short of time. Did she dare make another "announcement"? She took a deep breath. This was serious. "The prince—or most likely, the generals—are going to give up the siege on Stirling now that Cumberland is in Edinburgh. They'll be returning to Inverness and they'll be bringing their wounded from Falkirk." She rose to leave. "Call it what you will, but it will happen."

****

Ian stared at the empty door after Thea left. The lass truly was an enigma. They'd been having a spirited discussion—she probably thought it an argument, but Scots enjoyed bickering—about the Stuart lineage, and then she started spouting predictions of what was going to happen. In the future. Because she was from the future. Which, of course, was not possible. How could a lass with a clever mind—she clearly was intelligent and knew her history—be sane and rational one minute and the next sound utterly mad. If he were a more superstitious sort, he'd think the Seelies had sent someone from their Fae court to torment him.

He sat back in his chair. It could be possible that she wasn't really making predictions. It would make sense for the Jacobites to withdraw from Stirling and move west since Cumberland was in Edinburgh. Nothing really strange about that. Maybe Thea was simply making very, very astute calculations about both the English and Scottish armies. Cromartie did it all the time. So did the other generals. Just because she was a woman didn't mean she couldn't think like a man. Maybe things were done differently in Nova Scotia than here. Actually, come to think of it, after he'd heard from the messenger Ardsheal sent who explained the strategies of Murray and Drummond, the surprise attack at Falkirk sounded quite logical. Thea could have come to the same conclusion.

Except…how would she have known that was going to be their strategy?

The other possibility—a logical one, even though he didn't want to think about it, was that she was a spy. Arriving as she did at Hogmanay with a concocted story—well, one that he had quite helpfully initiated—had left lots of questions unanswered. Had she been sent by the English to secure a place for herself at Kilcoy to report back what training was taking place? She certainly hadn't sounded enthusiastic about backing the prince. She could have contacts waiting in Inverness… Why did she really want to go there as soon as possible? Ian shook his head. Being an English spy didn't make sense either. How would she have known about Scottish plans? And why would Hawley not have been warned if she had runners lurking about, ready to deliver messages?

Ian rubbed his temples. He was well on the way to life in a sanatorium himself.

"What did that Ross woman do to ye?"

Ian dropped his hands and opened his eyes as Cora entered the room, a scowl on her face.

"What do ye mean?"

"I saw her leave just now, and here ye are, looking as miserable as a cat left out in the rain." She rounded the desk, leaning across him to place her fingers on his forehead. "Let me rub the pain away."

Ian quickly became aware that Cora was all but sitting on his lap, her breasts dangerously close to his face. It was not a situation he wanted to be caught in and he pushed his chair back and stood. "Thank ye just the same, but I doona have a headache."

Undeterred, she moved closer and reached for him again. "I can make ye feel better," she practically purred as she pressed her body against his. "Just give me a chance."

He grabbed her hands and moved her arms down. "Ye ken this is nae appropriate."

"Ye didna used to mind my touch."

"What?" When he'd first come to Kilcoy, Cora had flirted with him almost outrageously, but not wanting to get involved with the daughter of the surgeon whom he had to work with and depend on, he'd always managed to brush off her advances. He'd certainly never encouraged her.

Her lower lip protruded. "'Tis that Ross woman, isn't it?"

Ian frowned. He couldn't deny that Thea intrigued him, but had his interest in her been that obvious? He thought he'd been careful. Best to put an end to this now, before Cora started spreading tales. "Miss Ross is a guest here, as I've told ye before. I've treated her with nothing but courtesy." Which was true, if he didn't include his fantasies. "Furthermore, Cora, I'd appreciate it if ye took the time to befriend her like Moire does."

Cora gave him a calculated look, one that he couldn't read. Then she smiled suddenly, which, for some reason, made him uneasy.

"Aye. I will befriend her if ye wish me too."

He nodded, relieved. "Thank ye." Then he remembered Callum's response to Thea. "It might be helpful if ye'd talk to your father as well. Miss Ross would like to help him when we receive wounded soldiers again, and it would be good if he welcomes her help rather than rejects it."

"I will definitely talk to my father," she replied, still smiling. "I'll go do so now."

Ian sat down after she left, glad that fixed the situation with Cora and her father. Thea would be pleased.

He picked up the stack of papers he'd been working on and started solving the problems of inventory and supplies.

Chapter Ten

Ian had acquiesced more quickly than Thea thought he would. It was less than forty-eight hours since she'd asked to be taken into Inverness, and here they were, about to have the sailboat dock in the harbor.

"They" included Moire and Cora, who had decided to come along with Ian and herself. That Moire wanted to go into town was expected, but it had been a surprise to see Cora waiting to board the boat as well. In the time Thea had been at Kilcoy, the girl had hardly been civil, and Thea generally avoided her. This morning, she was all smiles and had chattered—albeit it mostly to Moire—for nearly the entire crossing, although she'd had friendly words for Thea too. Perhaps Cora had finally accepted her. It would make things easier, especially when it came to working with her father, if a cordial relationship could be established.

Thea grinned. Better not to look a gift horse in the mouth and all that.

"What amuses ye?" Ian asked.

"Ah…just thinking." She'd been remembering that back on her parents' ranch, her dad always looked at a horse's mouth—actually, its teeth—to determine its age before buying it. She didn't think Cora would appreciate an inspection. What had made her grin, though, was how old the adage actually was. On her trip to Greece the year before, she'd discovered the saying dated back to a letter written by Saint Jerome to the people of Ephesus on the coast of Ionia in 400 AD. She was tempted to tease Ian by reciting ancient history, but then he might think she was really saying she'd lived back then too as well as in the future. The absurdity of the thought made her widen her grin.

Ian gave her a quizzical look. "Something strikes ye as humorous, else why are ye laughing?"

For a moment, an actual giggle threatened to bubble up, but she managed to squelch it and straightened her face. She didn't need to be giving Ian any more reasons for wondering if she was a lunatic. Or, for that matter, Moire or Cora either.

"I…was just thinking of how much I love being on the water." She raised her nose and sniffed the saltiness of the fresh air for good measure. "I've always liked to sail."

Ian narrowed his eyes slightly. She realized that women probably didn't do much sailing in the eighteenth century, so she added hastily, "In Nova Scotia, everyone learns how to sail since there aren't too many roads." She hoped that sounded plausible.

Whether it did or not, she wasn't sure, since Ian didn't answer, but he didn't pursue the subject, either. Instead, he gestured as the boat bumped against the dock. "Here we are."

"Yes, here we are," Moire said as a sailor lowered the plank and they disembarked. "While you and Thea purchase supplies, I want to buy some yardage and look at some new gowns." She turned to Cora. "Ye want to come with me and see what the merchants have brought in?"

"Um, nae. I would rather go with Ian and Thea since

they're wanting to add to my father's surgery." She glanced at Thea and then smiled at Ian. "I can be a big help to ye."

"Aye, that would be grand," Ian said with a big smile. "I'm sure Miss Ross will welcome that."

"Miss Ross" didn't need Cora's help, but Thea held her tongue. She wasn't quite sure why Cora seemed to have had a change of heart or why Ian was "welcoming" her suggestion, but it wasn't going to interfere with her getting the things she needed.

Their first stop was at the apothecary, which really didn't have many of the items she wanted since medicine had not advanced to embrace antiseptics like isoprophyl alcohol or hydrogen peroxide, nor had iodine been invented yet. She was able to get sphagnum moss, useful for padding wounds, while Cora purchased routine supplies like bandages.

Cora eyed her package as they walked outside. "Is that all ye're going to get?"

"No. I need to go to the general store to get some cider vinegar—"

"What are ye going to do with that?"

Ian was watching her with a wary look so she had to be careful how to explain its antibacterial use. "Back in Nova Scotia, it was used by the Mi'Kmaq to prevent infections."

"My father never heard of that," Cora said.

Because bacteria hadn't been discovered as a source of infection yet. But there was no reason to impart that bit of information. Thea smiled. "The native people had their own remedies."

"What else will ye need?" Ian asked.

"I'd like to go to the glassblower's shop next and get

some seaweed ash." Thea then quickly went on, "It's useful as a poultice to keep wounds clean."

Cora narrowed her gaze. "How do ye ken that?"

"Well, Nova Scotia is surrounded by water and seaweed, so it was natural for the natives to use it," Thea replied, "but when I went to Athens I learned that the Greeks and Romans had used the ash residue in soaps and soaked wet bandages in it." When Ian raised a brow, she added, "I learned that in the museums I visited."

He looked somewhat skeptical, but he didn't beleaguer the point. "What else?"

"I'd like to visit a perfumery, if you have one."

Ian crinkled his forehead. "I think there's a shop that sells sachets and things at the market off Church Street. Ye can try there."

Small bowls of flower petals sat on tables in the shop, which smelled deliciously of dried herbs as well. It reminded Thea of the shop she ran back in Texas, except she had a few New Age items also. She smothered a laugh. "New Age" had an entirely different meaning in the eighteenth century than it had in the twentieth and twenty-first.

An attractive lady with beautiful auburn hair came out from the back room. She gave Cora an appraising look, then smiled briefly at Ian before turning her attention to Thea. "My name is Bridgid. How can I help ye?"

Thea asked for lavender, witch hazel, and a few other herbs, which all were in stock, for which she was thankful. As the woman began to prepare the items, she gave another cursory glance toward Cora, who stood by the doorway with a frown on her face. Thea had the feeling the lady wanted to say something but had decided not to.

"If ye will wait a minute," the lady said after she'd put the wrapped parcels on the counter, "I think I have something else that ye may need."

Thea nodded, as the lady disappeared behind the curtain, wondering why the woman would think she needed anything else. Perhaps she'd guessed that what Thea had purchased were things used for healing? People who ran plant and herbal shops—at least in the twenty-first century—were often intuitive since they were attuned to nature.

She reemerged a moment later with a small white heather plant in a pot. "I think ye'll be able to use this." She smiled. "Nae charge, of course."

White heather, much more rare than purple, was a symbol for good luck. The woman must be intuitive after all. "Thank you. I appreciate it."

The sunlight was nearly blinding after the dimness in the shop, and Thea blinked several times to adjust her eyes, then turned back to thank the lady once more, but Bridgid was gone.

"Ye want to make perfume?" Cora asked snidely, diverting her attention. "We've nae need of such at Kilcoy."

"I don't need actual perfume." Thea ignored the tone of condescension in Cora's tone. "I just needed these items, especially the lavender and witch hazel."

"Why?" Her tone turned suspicious.

How much to say? Both had astringent, antimicrobial properties, but trying to explain that was sure to get her a censored look from Ian. "They can both help keep a wound from festering."

"Did ye learn that from those people in Nova Scotia

too?" Cora asked.

"The Mi'Kmaqs?" Thea dipped her chin in what she hoped looked like a nod since she had no idea of who had discovered those benefits. "Ummm."

Cora's eyes narrowed again. "Are they witch doctors, then?"

Thea started. "No! Of course not. They…they were the people who were already living there."

"They use things my father never heard of." Cora glanced toward Ian. "That old hag Maggie did too. A witch, some said—"

"Cora." Ian's voice was firm. "There are nae witches."

She shrugged. "'Twas before ye came. She was to be burned, but she managed to escape." She glanced at Thea before giving Ian a wide-eyed, innocent look. "Some said she had a familiar—a cat—that warned her."

"'Tis nonsense." Ian frowned at Cora. "I'm surprised ye'd repeat such gibberish."

Thea thought of Edie and the hair at her nape began to rise. The cat had attached herself to Thea when she'd first arrived. That wasn't unusual since most animals immediately liked her, but the cat was also black. She wasn't superstitious, but this was the eighteenth century, and it hadn't been all that long ago that witch hunts still happened.

Ian might consider Cora's remark nonsense, but was the girl calling her a witch?

Thea felt goosebumps form on her arms beneath the wool cape she wore and she clutched the pot, remembering that white heather was also for protection. Was she going to need it?

****

"Ye want to do what?" Ian asked Thea two days later when she approached him after they'd broken their fast.

"I need to gather some acorns and pine needles."

He drew his brows together. "Why?"

"To add to my medical supplies."

"I thought ye bought all of that in Inverness."

Thea gave him a rather exasperated look. "I got the things I couldn't find in nature. Now I need to collect the rest. Since we've had a thaw and snow melt, this is a good time to find the acorns."

"I planned to take the men slogging through the muddy conditions today as a training exercise."

"You don't have to accompany me. I'm sure Moire would enjoy a ride since it's not too cold."

He shook his head. "Moire can nae protect ye."

"I'm not going to venture far." Thea frowned. "I don't need protection."

Protection aside, Moire would quite likely decide to venture off somewhere as a lark since she chafed at being confined to the castle area and, from what he'd learned of Thea's own independent streak, she'd likely think it was a grand adventure too. "I vowed to Cromartie that Moire would be escorted at all times—"

"But you didn't promise Cromartie anything about me," Thea interrupted.

"Nae, but I brought ye here, so ye are under my protection."

Thea's eyes widened and she opened her mouth to retort, then snapped it shut. A look of confusion crossed her face. "I really don't need your protection."

"But ye have it anyway." The words were hardly out of his mouth when he realized he meant every one of them. Thea remained an enigma, since once, years ago when he fancied himself in love, the lass had betrayed him. He'd vowed never to let himself feel like that about another woman. But in the weeks since Thea arrived, he'd become increasingly attracted to her. It wasn't just lust, although he couldn't deny that ranked high on his list. Her figure was gently curved in all the right places, and her mouth, with its luscious full lips, was made for kissing. When she chewed her lip, it drove him to distraction. With her moonlight-colored hair and eyes so light blue they looked almost silvery, she did have an ethereal air about her, almost like one of the Fae. It made her look fragile, although she'd proved to be quite sturdy—sailing and riding astride weren't qualities most women were accomplished in. But there was something more. He had an overwhelming urge to protect her. He wasn't about to let her go wandering around the countryside unescorted. Whether she thought so or not, a woman alone was vulnerable. She didn't even know the terrain…

"I really do need to gather the acorns while I can find them before it snows again and I need to get the pine needles and bark too, so I can make salves and tinctures, which take a while to set." She gave him a hesitant look. 'We need to be ready for when the wounded arrive."

He blinked. His enigma was back to predicting again. "I've nae had any messages that the Jacobites are withdrawing from Stirling."

"They will be here within a fortnight."

The way she said it, calmly as if it were a fact already established, raised his wariness again, but he held his peace. Time would tell and, if he were right and the prince stayed at Stirling, that would put an end to all this predicting. For the present, he needed to give her another answer. "I canna let ye go out alone."

She sighed. "So then have one of the stable boys escort me."

As if a stable boy would do much good. The ones who hadn't gone with Ardsheal were practically still wet behind the ears. "They offer no protection, lass. They're too young."

Clearly exasperated, she chewed her lip, and Ian had to restrain himself from reaching for her. He'd no doubt get a resounding slap across his face and a justified one at that. But did she have to dart her tongue out the corner of her mouth too? He'd like to taste that particular spot...

"I have an idea, then," she said, bringing him out of his reverie.

He gave himself an inward shake to clear his head. "What?"

"Well, since you want to take your men on a training exercise in the mud and I need an escort, they can help me gather what I need." She grinned mischievously. "A whole company of soldiers should be ample protection, I would think. I'll go change my clothes."

Ian could only stare after her as she left.

****

"How did ye convince Ian to do this?" Moire asked a short time later as they stood and watched several dozen men practically crawling along the ground, picking up acorns near the forest line behind the castle.

"Hmmm. Well." She'd somewhat taken matters into her own hands, sneaking off toward the barracks after she'd changed clothes. By the time Ian realized where she was, he was too late. Thea stifled a grin. Sometimes, it was beneficial to have a friend who wrote romance novels. Thea had taken a page from one of those books to convince the soldiers she needed "help." An actual giggle threatened to erupt as she remembered Ian's expression when she told him the men had agreed to help her pick acorns and pine sprigs. She hadn't mentioned to him she'd promised them all a nice, hot tea from the needles, amply fortified with a bottle of whisky she'd procured from the study.

She managed to shrug nonchalantly. "Ian said the men needed practice in muddy conditions."

Moire laughed. "I suspect he meant having them charge at each other and physically end up rolling around in the muck."

"I think the men preferred my alternative." Thea didn't mention their reward. She glanced over to where Ian stood, regarding his men with an expression she couldn't read from where she stood. "I hope Ian isn't too upset with the change in plans."

Moire laughed again. "I think he's too flummoxed to be upset."

Thea wasn't sure what to say. She hoped she hadn't made him angry but, if she were honest with herself, she'd had another reason for marshalling his troops—so to speak—apart from needing the acorns and pine. She'd bristled a bit about his telling her she couldn't go out alone, but she'd been flummoxed herself when he'd also said she was under his protection because he'd brought her here. He'd probably just meant it was his duty to make sure she was safe, but no one—not even Alan— had ever said he would protect her. Not that she found Alan at fault. They'd practically grown up together and had always treated each other as equals.

Twenty-first-century women were independent and certainly didn't need a chauvinistic man telling them what they could or could not do. But there was something about a man saying he would protect her that was almost chivalrous, like one of King Arthur's knights. She shook her head. Clearly, she'd been reading too many of Charlotte's novels.

But…did she want that? She didn't know.

Chapter Eleven

"I think we're finally done," Moire said as she scraped bits of herbs from the table and put them in a pouch. "Unless ye want to go foraging again?"

"No, I think I have enough." Thea walked to the pantry and eyed the neatly arranged jars, tins, and pouches lining several shelves. "These should last a while."

"I hope so." Moire brushed her hands together and took off her apron. "I think I'm ready to go for a ride and get some fresh air."

"That sounds like a good idea," Thea answered. She'd spent the last ten days busily preparing tinctures that needed time to develop their potency. Moire offered to help with making the salves and putting together dry poultices that would only need to be soaked at the time they were needed. Cora, while she declined to help, often stuck around watching the proceedings, which made Thea somewhat uneasy, although she didn't know why. The girl hadn't been critical, simply observant. Moire had shrugged off Thea's concerns, saying Cora's presence was a good thing so she could explain to her father what they were doing. Being an optimist, Thea hoped that was true, but a sense of wariness remained.

Perhaps the reason had more to do with Ian than it did with her. Cora didn't hide her interest in the man, usually managing to sit next to him at dinner. Thea had lost count—not that she was counting—the number of times each night that Cora managed to brush Ian's hand or arm while passing food. Many of those times, her touch lingered, not that Thea kept count of those either. Cora heaped compliments on him for an accomplishment that he might casually mention and sat wide-eyed and smiling at comments he gave. For his part, Ian seemed not to notice the flirtation, instead turning his questions to Thea. Moire had remarked that Cora was probably jealous of the attention Ian gave her.

Thea had nearly laughed aloud at that. She was no femme fatale. She'd never had a boyfriend besides Alan. She didn't even know how to flirt and couldn't imagine acting like Cora did, either. Besides, she knew the real reason Ian focused on her, and it had nothing to do with romantic notions.

He still didn't believe she was from the future and was trying to find a logical explanation for why she was here. Thea sighed. She couldn't share that information.

She hung her apron on a hook in the kitchen. "Let's go see who's available to escort us on a ride."

To her surprise, Ian was just leading his own horse out when they got there. He raised a brow. "Are the two of ye planning to go somewhere?"

Moire wrinkled her nose at him. "Does it nae look like it?"

"Aye, it does," he replied, not changing his facial expression, "but I doona have anyone available right now to go with ye."

"Then we'll ride with ye." Moire gave him a bright smile and added, before he could protest, "Thea and I have been working inside most of the day and we're tired of smelling salves and tinctures. We need some fresh air."

Ian looked from her to Thea and then back. "I'm just going to ride the ridge to make sure all is well."

"'Tis fine with me." Moire glanced at Thea. "How about ye? It's a pretty view from the ridge."

"That sounds fine, if we aren't keeping Ian from work."

"Doona fash about that." Moire winked. " I doubt there are any Campbells or Sutherlands lurking about."

Thea tried not to appear startled. Those were the last names of Charlotte and Vi…She gave herself an inward shake. Moire couldn't know that. Campbell and Sutherland were also the surnames of government supporters and, while the Campbell seat was in Argyll, John Campbell, 4th Earl Loudoun, was stationed at nearby Fort George and Clan Sutherland lived north of the Black Isle. She turned to Ian. "Are you expecting trouble?"

"Nae, but 'tis better to be sure all is clear."

A few minutes later, they were on their way. Thea had to admit it was good breathing in fresh air after the confines of the small room in the cellar where they'd done most of the work. The relatively mild temperature—thanks to an unusually sunny day, rare for Scotland, this time of year—helped as well. She felt tight muscles begin to relax and loosened her reins, allowing her horse to follow Ian's up the slope to the top of the ridge.

When Ian's mount halted abruptly, Thea's mare skittered to one side to avoid plowing into the other's rump. Thea gathered the reins quickly, bringing her under control. "Sorry," she said as Ian frowned. "I wasn't paying attention."

He just shook his head and pointed. Thea followed his direction and her mood switched rapidly. In the distance, hundreds of men, like so many ants, were advancing toward them.

"What is it?" Moire asked coming alongside and looking down. "What's happening? Who are they?"

Thea felt Ian's gaze bore into her. She took a deep breath. "That would be the Jacobite army. They've abandoned the siege at Stirling."

****

As Ian viewed the troops pouring into the area behind the castle, he tried not to think about Thea's earlier prediction that the Jacobites would be coming to Inverness. It could have been a strategic guess that they would move north because Cumberland had, but most women, with the exception of Anne Mackintosh—the only female colonel in the entire army—weren't interested in military strategies.

Then again, Athena Ross didn't exactly fit the mold of "most" women. He'd found a book on Greek mythology in the study and done some reading on her namesake. Thea was aptly named, and not just because she looked like an ethereal goddess or because he was more intrigued with her than he'd ever been with any other female. The Greek Athena had been peace-minded, much like Thea, offering the olive branch to Poseidon after she won their contest, but Athena was also the goddess of wisdom, a trait his Thea also had. Not that she was *his* Thea, but—and this was what jolted him when he saw the troops advancing—Athena was also known for military victory, having aided the Achaeans in the Trojan War. His Thea seemed to know a lot about war also, even if she wasn't advocating fighting in this one. But how did it all fit together? It wasn't possible that she was from the past any more than it was possible she was from the future. The only thing that was definitely possible was that he was driving himself barmy.

The object of his barminess walked toward him from the surgery where the wounded men had been taken. She wore a grim expression.

"Are there many seriously hurt?" he asked as she came to stand beside him.

"Not as many as I thought, thank goodness."

He raised a brow. "Then why are ye so glum?"

She frowned. "A few have serious injuries and Callum won't let me near them."

He wasn't particularly surprised. The man was overly proud of his skills and certainly wouldn't want to be outdone by a woman. In Ian's mind, that made him a bit of an eejit, since women had been taking care of bairns' scrapes and bruises throughout the ages as well as binding their husbands' wounds. Still, Ian had to be careful not to run the man off. His cousin Ardsheal would have his head, to say nothing about Cromartie.

"Is there something ye would do differently than what's being done?"

She gave him an exasperated look. "Why do you think I've spent the last week and a half preparing all those remedies?"

"Mayhap ye could give some of them to Callum to use?"

"He would have to know what each is for and what dosage is needed," she said, "but he won't listen to me."

That didn't surprise Ian either. Callum would think anyone untrained wouldn't know more than he did. "I'll go talk to him."

"Before you do…"

Thea chewed her lip and, for a moment, he was distracted. What was it about that gesture that aroused his lust? All he wanted to do was lean down and capture that luscious lip with his own, then delve deep into her mouth…

"Well?" she asked.

He realized she must have finished her sentence while he was allowing himself to be distracted. Again. "What were ye saying?"

She sighed. "I was asking if you'd explain to Callum that he must use whisky to cleanse the wounds that are festering."

Ian stared at her. "Ye want to pour good whisky on a wound? Wouldn't it be better to let the man drink it to dim the pain?"

"That's fine, too, but whisky is alcohol and alcohol is an antiseptic—"

"A what?"

"An anti— Something that will destroy germs—"

"What are those?"

Thea sighed again. He'd evidently forgotten a previous conversation about germs, or maybe he hadn't been listening. "Germs haven't been discovered yet, but they and bacteria…" She held up a hand before he could ask the obvious question. "Bacteria hasn't been discovered yet either, but both are what cause a wound to become infected. The alcohol will clean it and let it heal."

Ian was quiet for a moment, trying to phrase his next question carefully. "Where did ye hear that?"

"I…read about it. Alan was studying to be a physician."

Alan. Her husband. Understanding suddenly broke through and Ian felt elated at the relief. If her husband had studied—more intensely than Callum—then her unusual knowledge would make sense. There wasn't anything strange about it if it were some new theory that Callum hadn't heard of.

He smiled. "Did your husband study at Edinburgh or on the Continent?"

She shook her head. "Neither. He was at the University of Texas."

Texas. Ian's elation drained away like water in a sieve. Thea was back to talking about the future. One that didn't exist.

But how could he convince her it didn't?

****

Thea could see in Ian's eyes the exact moment when he decided—once more—that she was addled in the head. Not only did his genial smile disappear but an expression of wariness crossed his face and his eyes went blank, as if he shuttered himself from her. Not that he said anything. Was he hesitant to speak for fear it might set her off in some wild rant or nonsensical antics? Perhaps nonsensical was the wrong word to use, since he obviously didn't think her talk of the future made any sense to begin with. Right now, though, the important thing was to get those soldiers treated with the medical supplies she'd purchased.

"I don't care what you tell Callum about where Alan studied as long as you can convince him to use my remedies."

Ian shook his head. "I doona think anyone could convince him to pour good whisky away. He is a Scot, ye ken."

And a stubborn one, but Thea held her peace on that opinion. "All right, then. At least, he should use the witch hazel. It's an astringent—"

"A what?"

Thea suppressed a sigh. He didn't recall that part of the conversation either. "An astringent also helps prevent infections."

"'Tis strange terms ye use. Callum will argue he's never heard of them."

Which would actually be true, but that didn't excuse the man from being a male chauvinist prig. Thea held her opinion on that too. "Ye can just say that those terms are words for new experiments that have recently been tested and proved to help." When Ian still looked doubtful, she added, "If even one of those soldiers should die because of an infection that could have been prevented, how would you feel?"

Ian frowned. "I am nae a physician—"

"No, but if you don't say something to Callum, you will be responsible." She hated having to guilt Ian, but he was wavering. She wouldn't be pressing the point, but men's lives could be saved by what she knew would work, if she could just get him to believe her. "Please. Even one life is too many to lose."

His face set. "All right, lass. I'll talk to Callum."

"Thank you!"

On impulse, she threw her arms around his neck and raised on tiptoe to kiss his cheek. Startled, he turned his head and her mouth brushed across his. Time froze for an instant. Then his hands encircled her waist, drawing her closer as his lips pressed against hers. They were warm, gentle yet firm, angling across hers as if asking for permission to deepen the kiss. The exquisite feel of his tongue probing lightly against her mouth was irresistible and she opened to him. Thea experienced a moment of lightheadedness. Strange sensations flashed through her body, making her tingle in places that she didn't know could tingle as his tongue expertly filled her mouth, making her want more…

A door slammed behind them and Thea jumped like a startled deer, unbalancing herself. Ian righted her before slowly dropping his hands and turning around.

Cora stood there, glaring angrily at Thea. Ian raised a brow, but before he could say anything, she stomped off.

"I guess we made her upset," Thea said in a somewhat shaky voice.

Ian shrugged. "'Tis of nae matter."

Thea opened her mouth, then closed it. She wasn't sure if he meant Cora's reaction was of no matter or if their kiss wasn't all that big a deal to him. She had instigated it, after all. Perhaps it was better that she didn't ask, because she wasn't sure she wanted to know the answer.

Chapter Twelve

"So have ye discovered anything about the mysterious Athena Ross?" his cousin asked as he accepted a whisky from Ian and sat back in the armchair by the study's hearth.

It was the question Ian had been dreading ever since Ardsheal had shown up this morning. What could he say about a woman who kept insisting she was from the future? And who was oddly accurate in predicting some of the events that had happened? Even mentioning something like that could be dangerous for Thea. Witch hunts may have been banned, but many people still attributed anything they couldn't explain—like foretelling the future—to witchery. His cousin wasn't a superstitious man who believed in that kind of nonsense, but he still might have Thea carted off to insure no uprising might occur here. After the kiss they'd shared, even though it was spontaneous, he had an even stronger urge to protect her.

"Nothing new," he replied. "She said her parents moved to Nova Scotia where she married another Scot and they returned here so he could study medicine, only he was killed." He didn't add that this was three years ago or her claim about where her husband studied medicine. However, since he didn't want Ardsheal to start asking specific questions, he hurriedly went on. "According to the lass, the escort she'd hired to take her to the coast absconded with her money and her belongings." Better to stick with the original story they'd invented rather than get tangled in a web of more lies.

His cousin studied him. "And ye believe her?"

Ian managed to hold his cousin's gaze. "Her story makes sense, I think."

"Nae precisely what I asked." Ardsheal put his glass down. "She's nae given any cause for concern, then?"

Thea had given him plenty of personal causes through the unusual conversations they'd had, to say nothing of his growing desire for her, which was a danger itself. The kiss proved that. Instead of brushing it off, once he'd tasted the sweetness of her lips, he'd deepened it. No woman had ever felt so right in his arms. Even the woman who'd betrayed him hadn't felt this *right*. The softness of her curves had fit perfectly against him. If Cora hadn't interrupted them… But this was not something he would share. He shook his head. "The lass has been most helpful. She's even got some theories about curing infections that her husband learned about." Where she'd gotten those theories was another area he wouldn't wander into right now.

His cousin raised a brow. "What does Callum think about that?"

"He wasn't overly enthusiastic." That was putting it as mildly as Ian could. When he'd approached Callum regarding what Thea had told him, the man spit on the floor and said he'd never heard of such things as germs and bacteria, let alone the solutions that Thea suggested. Furthermore, he'd been adamant that she not set a foot inside his surgery.

"Well, make sure ye doona rile the man. We will need him in the days to come."

Ian sensed a note of worry in his cousin's voice and grasped the opportunity to change the subject, since it created a direct dilemma for him.

"Do ye anticipate trouble?"

"'Twould be foolish nae to anticipate trouble," Ardsheal answered, "especially after the narrow escape our prince just had."

Ian's ears perked up. "Escape? What has happened?"

His cousin got up and went to refill his whisky before answering. "First, let me fill ye in on what happened after we received word that Cumberland had come to Edinburgh." He took his seat. "The generals decided to divide the army into two segments, one without heavy artillery, that could advance more quickly in case Cumberland decided to attack. Those were the men, mostly lowlanders, that Murray brought up through Perth and Dundee. They also included the walking wounded that arrived here. The prince decided to march with the Highlanders and artillery through Dunkeld and Atholl. I was with him. We stopped at Castle Menzie on February fourth and reached the pass at Killecrankie on the sixth. The prince was travelling incognito. When he heard about General Gordon forcing the surrender of Ruthven Barracks at Badenoch, he decided to go there to congratulate the general in person."

"Wasn't that risky?" Ian asked.

His cousin shrugged. "It didna seem so at the time, since Cumberland was still in Edinburgh. Things changed, though, when we got to Moy Hall a few days later."

"Moy Hall? Why did the prince want to go there?"

"As ye ken, the lady of the manor, Anne

Mackintosh, supports the cause and the prince is appreciative of her efforts. He took a contingent of fifty men to go ahead and warn her that half the army was coming," his cousin answered. "Moy Hall is a good location to wait for Cumberland to advance. It's close enough to Inverness to attack after the troops were rested and far enough away for them not to be detected. Or so we thought."

"What happened?"

"Apparently, someone along the way who recognized the prince—or maybe a turncoat in our midst—sent word to Loudoun in Inverness that the prince was nearby."

"Since ye didna announce this as soon as ye arrived, I assume the prince avoided capture?" Ian asked wryly.

"Aye. Thanks to a lassie working at the Horns Inn who overheard Loudoun's men talking about their plans. She sent word to Lady Anne's mother-in-law who, in turn, sent one of her young runners to Moy Hall."

"And the prince was long gone by the time the English showed up?"

Ardsheal grinned. "The Redcoats never made it to the hall."

Ian raised both brows. "Prince Charlie stood his ground with only fifty soldiers?"

"Nae. The prince was roused and left with his men. 'Twas Anne who stood her ground…and with only six men."

"What?"

"Aye." His cousin's grin widened. "I found out later, when I returned, that she and her blacksmith devised a plan to wait for the Redcoats at the narrow pass Craig an Eoin. They set up stacks of peat and hid behind them.

Thankfully, it was a cloudy night and, to the advancing troops, it looked like men blocking the road."

Ian gave him a puzzled look. "A few men wouldn't have deterred the English, though."

"True, but when the Redcoats were about two hundred feet away, the blacksmith and two others started shouting to MacDonalds and Camerons to form left and right while the Mackintoshs took the center. Then…" His cousin grinned again. "…they moved from place to place firing muskets at each interval and banging swords on rocks, which gave the English the impression that the rest of the prince's army had actually arrived."

Ian widened his eyes. "And the Redcoats turned back?"

"Aye." Ardsheal said. "Fifteen hundred men defeated by half a dozen Scots. Nae bad for odds, I would say."

"I would tend to agree. I'm sure the prince was pleased when he heard of the rout."

"That he was." Ardsheal finished his whisky. "But he was even more pleased that the English didn't stop at Inverness but continued running into Sutherland."

"So only a few soldiers are left at Fort George?"

His cousin nodded. "The prince intends to attack within days and destroy the fort so the English can't return."

"Sounds like a wise decision."

Ardsheal smiled. "That's just the beginning of what the prince intends to destroy, but I canna go into more detail right now."

"I understand. Are ye going to be taking over Kilcoy Castle now that ye're back?"

"Nae. I'm going back to field headquarters." His

cousin stood. "I just wanted ye to ken how matters stood." He walked to the door, then turned back. "Be sure the Ross lass does nothing to run off Callum. We may need him."

****

Thea watched from the solar window as Ardsheal rode away. "I wonder what news he brought," she said to Moire, who stood beside her.

Moire waved a hand nonchalantly. "More than likely, just an update about the troops and what they'll need in way of supplies and ammunition. Ian's cousin was in charge of all that before he left to join the prince, so now all that is up to him."

"Besides training new recruits," Thea said.

"Well, that too. Ardsheal probably wanted to know how many of them were ready to join the army."

Thea turned from the window. "This war is so senseless."

Moire's eyes widened. "Ye best nae say that out loud."

"Why not? It's not like I'm saying I'm on the English side of this. I don't want blood shed on either side."

"'Tis nae something men think about, though."

"Well, they should," Thea replied. "A lot of men are going to die soon."

Moire frowned. "What do ye mean?"

Thea bit her lip. She needed to be careful that she didn't say something that would sound absurd...or insane. "Cumberland will eventually attack."

"We doona ken that for certain."

Thea refrained from rolling her eyes. "I don't think Cumberland came to Edinburgh for the warm weather,

117

do you?"

"Nae, but the king could have sent him up here as a sort of warning."

"Exactly," Thea said, "but his presence will not be just a warning if the prince keeps amassing more soldiers and starts attacking the English holdings."

"Well, he withdrew from the siege at Stirling."

"Only because Cumberland moved north." Thea looked at Moire. "The duke will see Prince Charlie amassing his forces here as a threat."

"I doona think we can do anything about that."

"Maybe we can. Do you think you could write to your father, or even your uncle, and ask if there's any chance the prince would be willing to discuss a peace treaty?"

Moire shook her head. "Ye doona understand. The men who fight for the prince believe a Stuart belongs on the throne. That King James should never have been exiled and his daughter allowed to ascend the throne because she is Protestant. And certainly not that a Dutch prince be allowed to co-rule. Even though the massacre at Glen Coe happened nearly sixty years ago, Scots have long memories. And now, because neither Queen Mary nor Queen Anne had children, we have another foreigner on the throne."

"And you believe that a Stuart should be returned even if it means thousands of men will die?"

"I doona want to see men die, either." Moire hesitated. "I'm nae sure it matters what I think. Or ye, for that matter. We are women. Who would listen to us?"

Unfortunately, what Moire said was true. Even in the twenty-first century, it was still harder for women to advance in politics and as heads of corporations than it was for men. And this was the eighteenth century where women were still considered chattel. If her friend Vi were here, she'd probably manage to lead a rally for women's rights, at least to be heard. Thea sighed. "I suppose you are right. I can't even get Callum to listen to my ideas of preventing infections."

Moire grimaced. "He's hardheaded."

"That's putting it mildly," Thea answered. "Ian even talked to him about just hearing me out. He still said no."

"Maybe Ian could talk to him again?"

Thea shook her head. "I don't know that it would do any good. I decided, though, that when the next batch of wounded men come in, I'll start tending them myself. I don't need to go into Callum's surgery to do it."

Moire nodded. "That may be the way to go about it. Just don't tell Ian."

"I won't." Thea smiled. "If men won't listen to us, we don't need to listen to them.'

****

Ian heard the last part of that conversation as he passed by the solar. If there was one thing he didn't need to hear, particularly after his cousin's parting words to make sure the surgeon stayed at Kilcoy, it was that Thea was going to directly oppose Callum by treating soldiers herself. He inhaled deeply and entered the room.

Moire hurried past him to the door. "I need to check with Mrs. Moffett about something," she said and fled the room. Thea watched her, then turned her attention to Ian, looking resigned.

"How much did you hear?"

"Enough." At least, the lass wasn't going to attempt to hide her intentions. "Ye canna set up a second surgery."

She shook her head. "I'm not planning to. I can use my remedies anywhere."

"Nae quite the point I wanted to make." He took another deep breath. "Callum will see it as defiance."

Thea shrugged. "It will be me defying him. I really don't care what he thinks."

Generally, Ian admired anyone who stuck to their beliefs and he respected the fact that Thea believed in what she wanted to do, but with the war moving closer, he couldn't afford to lose his surgeon. His cousin was right about that.

"I canna allow it."

Thea straightened her shoulders and lifted her chin. The look she gave him could have frozen water in midsummer. "I will not allow someone to die if I can prevent it. And I can prevent it."

She crossed her arms under her breasts which made them lift and jut, causing Ian to momentarily forget the subject at hand.

"I can save lives."

Ian blinked, forcing himself to refocus. "What?"

"I said, I can save lives. So whether you give me permission or not, that is what I am going to do."

He frowned. He was not used to having his orders questioned, let alone having a blatant refusal of them. The lass obviously had no fear of him. Not that he wanted her to fear him. Quite the opposite. He wanted her to… He shook his head to clear it of where his mind was going.

"You can shake your head all you want. I won't change my mind."

He blinked again. " I didna mean it that way."

She lifted a brow. "Then you agree with me?"

"I…didna say that." How could one woman confuse him so much? "I doona have a problem with you using your remedies, but I canna afford to have Callum leave because ye insult his skills."

"Men!" Thea looked heavenward and sighed. "All right. I'll wait, for now, since none of the current patients seem to be in danger. However, when we get casualties from the destruction of Fort George—"

"Fort George?" Had she somehow been listening at his study? But she'd been in the solar, not anywhere close… "Fort George?" he asked again. "What do ye mean by that?"

Thea gave him a steady look. "By the end of this month, the prince's generals will attack Fort George. Major Grant will surrender and the Jacobites will burn the fort to the ground so it cannot be used again by the English."

He stared at her. If there was a second thing he didn't need to hear since he'd come into the solar, it was this prediction…which was very likely to happen, according to his cousin.

But how did Thea know?

Chapter Thirteen

Ian leaned against one of the portico columns and looked over the quiet courtyard. The sun had long set, but the evening air wasn't all that cold, probably because the back of the castle was blocked from the wind. It didn't really matter, though. What he needed was some solitude and, with everyone inside milling about after a filling dinner, this was the place he could find it.

The siege and consequent destruction of Fort George had gone exactly as Thea had said it would. There had been few casualties because of the major's surrender, and he hadn't had to intervene between Thea and Callum, as her medicines weren't needed. But it was just a matter of time before new casualties would come in and he'd have to issue orders that probably neither one of them would like. Or maybe even obey. Callum wasn't used to anyone questioning his skills or judgment and, Ian suspected, Thea wasn't used to it either.

Which really brought to the surface his real concern. Thea wasn't like other women. His lust and desire for her aside, she didn't act like other women. She was an independent thinker, not afraid to voice her opinions or to stand up to him when she thought she was right. Most women would defer to authority. Thea didn't.

Was it possible that she really was from the twenty-first century? He'd been driving himself barmy denying it—any logical, sane person would—but what if it were really true? What if she knew what was going to happen because in her century it had already taken place? It was a completely wild theory, but he was beginning to think nothing else made sense either.

"Ye look troubled," Cora said.

Ian started. Allowing someone to sneak up on him could mean death. He drilled that into his men every single day. Yet here he was, oblivious to footfalls. He turned. "I was seeking solitude because I need to think."

"Doona let me disturb ye, then." Cora put a hand on his shoulder. "Ye just looked troubled at dinner, and I wanted to give ye comfort." She leaned against him. "I will be verra quiet if ye let me stay with ye."

Ian was quite aware that she'd managed to press her breast against his arm as she leaned into him. He shifted slowly, putting some space between them. "Ye should go inside. 'Tis getting cold."

Undeterred, she moved closer. "Ye can keep me warm, then."

How could he make himself clear without insulting the girl? Now, more than ever, because of the situation with Callum and Thea, he needed to be careful he didn't offend. "I'm sorry, but I really need to be alone so I can think. I've a problem I must solve." He gestured. "Go inside and get warm."

She pouted, narrowing her eyes. "It's that Ross woman, isn't it?"

Ian frowned. "What do ye mean?"

"Ever since she came, ye have been ignoring me."

"I haven't been ignoring ye." Good God! He'd not given Cora any thought at all. He couldn't say that, though, and he certainly wasn't going to discuss Thea. "My cousin gave me some news that I need to ponder."

He managed to smile. "I really need to concentrate on that. Ye understand that, nae?"

She pouted, and he wondered if she'd argue further, but then she seemed to think better of it and nodded her head. "I will be here for ye if ye need me."

"Thank ye. I'll remember." To his relief, she appeared satisfied with his answer and went back inside. He turned back to the empty courtyard.

Now he had one more problem to think about.

****

"The prince is pleased with the destruction of Fort George." Ian laid down the paper a messenger had just delivered from Ardsheal's camp and looked at Thea, seated across the desk from him. "'Tis good news for all of us."

"Yes, it is. But…" Her voice trailed off.

He gave her a calculated look. "Yes, but? What is it ye want to say?"

Thea took a deep breath. Fort George was a victory, but the Scots weren't going to win the war. If she were going to convince Ian to try and persuade the Jacobites to settle this mess peacefully, she'd have to go on a limb. Again.

"Did you know there is unrest stirring on the Greek Peloponnese peninsula that is similar to what is going on in Scotland?"

"I dinna." He hesitated. "Was this something ye heard when ye visited Athens?"

She nodded, preferring not to answer directly since she'd visited Athens in the twenty-first century and not the eighteenth.

"Word had it that Catherine the Great is envisioning becoming independent of the Ottoman Empire, much like your prince is with King George. She's even willing to split the empire with Empress Maria Theresa of Austria if they could bring power back to Constantinople."

Ian frowned. "We have heard nae word of this."

That was because it wasn't going to happen for another twenty-four years until Admiral Alexay Orlov of Russia would arrive on the peninsula in 1770, but the outcome was going to be the same. The uprising would be repressed, just like the Jacobite rebellion would be at Culloden. Ian would think her completely daft—or worse—if she started predicting other world events, though. "I think maybe Catherine's advisors are trying to talk her out of it since the timing didn't seem quite right." At least, the part of timing was true. Greece wouldn't achieve independence from the Ottomans until 1830. Best leave that unsaid too.

Ian quirked a brow. "Are ye trying to hint that Prince Charlie's timing isna right?"

She grimaced. "I think I've already said he should be willing to meet with King George and discuss a settlement of sorts."

Ian shook his head. "'Tis nae going to happen. A Prussian king will nae allow a Stuart to take back the throne."

"Even if it only involves Scotland and not Britain?"

"Even if it involves only one hectare. George willna give it up." He shrugged. "But, since ye are keen on this subject, what do ye think Cumberland's next move will be now that we've destroyed Fort George?"

She gave him a steady look. "He is going to move north to Aberdeen."

"Aberdeen? In the winter? Edinburgh is cold enough

for an Englishman."

"He'll want to be closer to assess the strength of the prince's army."

"Ye seem quite sure about this."

"I am."

Ian leaned back, giving her a thoughtful look. "Then we shall see what happens."

Thea blinked, trying to hide her surprise. Was Ian beginning to finally believe that she knew what she was talking about because she was from the future?

****

She still wasn't quite over her surprise when she met Moire in the solar a short time later. Ian's last statement was the first time she'd felt like he'd even considered that she might be telling the truth, as absurdly impossible as it seemed. Not that she blamed Ian. She wouldn't believe herself either if she hadn't experienced the weird journey.

"Ye seem lost in thought," Moire said.

She had been lost in thought, wondering again, for the zillionth time, how she'd managed to time-travel. She jolted herself back to the present…or back from the future, anyway. "Ian and I were having a bit of a disagreement earlier."

Moire's eyebrows went up. "About what?"

"Pretty much what we usually argue about. I think this war could end without more bloodshed if only both the king and the prince would agree to meet and discuss the possibility of a co-rule. Ian obviously didn't agree."

Moire shook her head. "'Tis because Ian is nae only a Scot but a Stuart. Ye ken that he's a distant cousin of the prince?"

Thea actually hadn't thought about that. Stuart was

a common name, similar to Smith or Jones in America, but then she probably shouldn't be surprised either since the clans had deep roots that went back to various invasions of Scotland, and descendants obviously felt strong ties. "Still. Wouldn't it be better if no more soldiers were killed on either side?"

Moire sighed. "Ye and I may think so, but 'tis nae the way men see things."

And that hadn't changed in future centuries either. Her world—the modern one—was experiencing conflicts in many countries, most of which could have been avoided if the various leaders weren't grasping for power. Those leaders might not be monarchs, but the outcome seemed to be the same. "Do you think nothing can be done, then?"

"I doona ken," Moire answered. "Nae all Scots want Charles Edward Stuart on the throne. Some doona think him a true Scot since he was nae born nor raised in Scotland."

Something she'd mentioned herself. "You told me a while back that brother is fighting against brother in some of our clans. Maybe if Ian could just get some of them—they're all Scots—to talk, it would help."

Moire shook her head again. "Ye doona understand, Thea. Ian is a Stuart. 'Twould nae only be treason—in his eyes—to go against the man he believes should be king, but 'twould be unloyal. Loyalty is the most important thing to a Scot."

Thea supposed Moire was right, but it was sad that Ian wouldn't listen to reason. Aside from the obvious fact that he was handsome and brawny, Ian was also intelligent and honest and treated his men fairly. Alan had those traits and they were ones she admired, although she had to admit to herself those weren't the only reasons she wanted Ian to understand her. She'd been trying to deny that she was attracted to him, but after the kiss they'd shared—which she'd meant only to be a thank you, but it had obviously been quite a bit more—there was no denying that she was attracted to him. Dangerously so, considering her circumstances. The chances of romance blooming were fantastical, more appropriate for one of Charlotte's novels than for her to even be considering.

And Culloden loomed. The thought that Ian might die in that battle was terrifying. She'd gone through that experience once. She didn't want to do it again.

Better to keep all thoughts of Ian on simply a practical level. It was much safer.

Chapter Fourteen

Ian carried the wounded man into the surgery, worrying more about stanching the man's bleeding than listening to the muffled sobs and explanations of the lad following him.

"Donald, I will deal with ye later. Right now, Artair needs tending."

"Aye," Callum agreed, coming to meet him. "Put him on the table."

Ian laid the moaning man gently down, not liking the amount of blood that stained the man's shoulder. "Will he be all right?"

"'Tis too early for me to say," Callum replied, ripping the torn shirt off and examining the wound. 'He's lost a lot of blood."

"'Twas nae my fault!" Donald sobbed behind them. "I didna ken the wrap on my sword would come undone."

"Later, Donald," Ian said and turned to Callum. "What can I do?"

"Ye can hold your hand right here." The surgeon placed Ian's hand over the wound. "Slow the bleeding if ye can while I get bandages."

"He needs a bandage." Thea strode swiftly toward them, a soggy, bunched cloth in her hand. "Let me see him."

"'Tis my patient," Callum all but snarled at her. "I

will tend him."

She pushed her way past him and lifted Ian's hand. "The wound's got dirt in it—"

"He fell and rolled on the ground after my sword struck him." Donald snuffled. "I didna mean—"

"Later, Donald." The lad was hardly old enough to shave. Ian frowned at him, then redirected his gaze to Callum. 'Let Miss Ross give her opinion."

The surgeon looked like a thunderstorm was going to break across his face, but he kept quiet.

"The wound needs to be cleaned first," Thea said. "I need whisky."

Callum stared at her. "Ye want to drink?"

"Not me," she answered, sounding aggravated. "It needs to be poured onto the wound to sterilize it."

"To what?" Callum asked.

She shook her head. "To clean it."

"I have water for that."

"It won't be enough. The dirt could already be affecting his blood."

"Nonsense. The wound bleeds freely," the surgeon answered. "What it needs is a bandage, which I will get."

Thea ignored him as he turned away and placed the soggy cloth she carried over the wound instead, pressing down hard with both hands.

"What are ye doing?" Ian asked.

"I'm applying a poultice with witch hazel. It helps stop the bleeding."

"Are ye sure?"

"I am. Please convince Callum that this will help."

Ian sighed. Convincing the man wasn't going to be easy since he didn't like his authority questioned. And he was right.

"Take that thing off," Callum said when he returned. "I already have enough bandages."

"This needs to stay on," Thea said. "Put your bandages over the top."

"Doona tell me—"

"What can it hurt, Callum?" Ian intervened. "It looks like there's nae blood draining now. It might start up again if the poultice is removed."

Callum gave him a dark look, but held his peace. He stepped closer to Thea and, for a moment, Ian was afraid there would be a physical altercation. His fists clenched in preparation. No one—not even the surgeon—was going to strike Thea. Or any woman, for that matter, but Thea was the one at whom Callum was directing his wrath. For her part, Thea didn't move either, staring the man down. Ian was beginning to wonder which of them was more stubborn.

The stalemate was broken when Artair moaned again. Thea stepped back. Callum gave her one last glare before turning his attention to bandaging the wounded man.

Ian leaned down to whisper in her ear, catching the scent of a spicy fragrance that came either from her hair or from the poultice she'd carried. He didn't know which, but it distracted him before he forced himself to refocus.

"Best ye leave now, lass, before another storm erupts."

She gave him a contemplative look and for a moment he thought she'd not follow his request, but then she nodded and turned away.

Ian breathed a sigh of relief. One crisis averted, but it probably wouldn't be the last.

He turned to Donald. "We'll talk in my study. Come along."

****

"I'm glad ye are back," Ian said to Malcolm Ross two days later as he poured him a whisky and took the seat behind his desk.

"I'd have come sooner, but the prince wanted me to find out how much activity was still happening at Balnagown Castle."

Ian nodded. The castle, in Easter Ross, was the clan seat for the Pitcalnie line of Rosses. As in so many families, Malcolm's father, Alexander, eighteenth chief, was a loyalist to King George, while his son fought for the prince. Alexander had also garrisoned Inverness Castle until recently. "What did ye find?"

"'Tis mostly only a small staff that remain," Malcolm replied. "Since Prince Charlie destroyed Fort George, my father's men fled north through Dornoch to Sutherland." He grimaced. "'Twas my uncle's idea."

Ian frowned as well. Malcolm's uncle was Duncan Forbes, Lord Culloden, who was also president of the Court of Session for King George. If he ordered the men to go north, they must have some kind of master plan. "Were ye able to find out why they went that far north?"

Malcolm shrugged. "I couldna find out for sure, but the blacksmith at Balnagown told me he overheard something about Cumberland wanting the men to regroup in a safe place so preparations could be made for the spring."

Ian felt the hair at his nape rise. Thea had said Cumberland would be moving north. She'd mentioned Aberdeen, which was a distance from Sutherland by road, but bringing troops south from there by ship would be much quicker. "I assume ye mean they're to be battle-ready, then?"

Malcolm raised a brow. "I doona think they're planning to negotiate a peace settlement, if that's what ye mean."

It wasn't, but he had to ask since Thea kept insisting that talks between the king and prince could avoid bloodshed. Now he had his answer. Cumberland might not personally be joining the men who'd fled north, but he could still make sure they were prepared. And—Ian's hair prickled again—those men were a lot closer to Inverness than the duke was at present.

"'Tis good for us to ken," he said. "I will send out the call for more men to train here on the Black Isle."

"Aye. 'Tis one of the things the prince wanted me to tell ye. Now," Malcolm put the empty whisky glass down and stood. "I'd best be getting back."

Ian stood too. "Just one more thing, before ye leave."

Malcolm paused. "What is it? More trouble?"

"Nae." Ian wasn't about to mention that the surgeon was still stewing about Thea invading his surgery two days ago. He'd handle that matter himself. "I was just wondering if ye kenned of a Ross family that moved to Nova Scotia with a bonny lass who returned recently." Ian really wasn't quite sure how recently it was, given all the strange circumstances. He gave Malcolm an abbreviated version of what had happened. "The lass's name is Athena. I thought ye might ken who she is."

"I've never heard of a lass by that name. 'Tis unusual. I'm sure I would remember it." Malcolm drew his brows together in thought, then shook his head. "I doona think she belongs to us."

Ian gave a resigned sigh. He really wasn't surprised. But it did add to the mystery—once again—of who Thea Ross really was.

****

"Artair is dead."

Thea stared at Ian, her blood chilling at those words, and set down the plate she'd just filled. It was a good thing she hadn't yet started eating her breakfast or she would have emptied the contents of her stomach in front of him. She grabbed the back of a chair in the small morning room.

"When?"

"Sometime before dawn." Ian looked grim. "Callum went to check on him and he was nae breathing."

She sank down onto the chair. "He seemed to be recovering when I saw him last evening."

Ian gave her a sharp look. "Did Callum ken ye saw Artair?"

Thea frowned. "I don't think so. The surgery was empty."

"'Tis good, then."

"Good?" Her frown deepened. "You think a man dying is good?"

"Nae. Artair was a fine soldier." He shook his head. "I meant 'tis good Callum didna see ye."

Her skin began to prickle. "Why?"

Ian walked to the door and poked his head into the hallway before he came back to the table and lowered his voice. "Because he thinks ye are responsible for Artair's death."

"What?"

"Shhh. We doona need anyone hearing ye," Ian said.

Thea took a deep breath to calm herself. "Why

would he think that?" She managed to control her tone. "I tried to help Artair! I'm the one who put the poultice on to stop the bleeding!" When Ian didn't reply, another chill ran through her. "What is it you aren't telling me?"

He hesitated, glancing toward the door once more and then leaned down to practically whisper in her ear. If the situation hadn't been so dire, she would have reveled in his closeness. Now, though, his nearness only made every fiber of her being set on edge.

"He thinks whatever ye put on the poultice is what killed Artair."

"What?" She clapped a hand over her mouth and glanced toward the door too before managing to lower her voice. "How can he say that? If this death were anyone's fault, it should be his. He didn't allow me to cleanse the wound properly. Water wouldn't get all the dirt out. Artair probably died from sepsis."

"From what?"

"Sepsis. It happens when the blood gets poisoned by foreign matter. Like dirt." She pursed her lips. "The poultice was only witch hazel, which helps stop bleeding."

"Callum said he never heard of such a thing."

Thea tried to control her rapidly rising fury. "Just because he hasn't heard of it doesn't mean it doesn't work." She huffed a breath. "It is commonly known in the twenty-first century."

This time Ian put his hand over her mouth. "Ye have got to stop talking like that." He removed his hand. "'Tis dangerous."

"Because someone will think I'm mad?"

"Being considered barmy would be a better outcome."

"What do you mean by that?"

Ian hesitated again, then lowered his voice once more. "Because right now, Callum thinks ye are a witch."

Thea stared at him. "You cannot be serious."

"I wish I were nae. Cora has been telling him things about ye kenning what's going to happen next… She probably overheard some of our conversation." He shook his head. "I told him there are nae witches, but he just snorted and said Janet Horne was probably nae the last one."

Janet Horne. Thea shuddered involuntarily. She knew the story since the eighteenth-century magistrate involved in the whole horrible mess had been a Ross. Janet was considered "strange," although in modern times she'd probably have been diagnosed with dementia. Her daughter had been born with club feet that made them look like hooves and the locals accused Janet of trying to turn her into a pony to ride so she wouldn't have to walk. The outcome had been gruesome. Janet was tarred, feathered, and paraded in a barrel throughout Dornoch before she was burned at the stake.

"But the Witchcraft Act of 1736 banned all that." Thea lifted her chin with false bravado. "Surely someone like Callum knows that."

Ian watched her silently for a moment, then he shook his head. "Laws doona change a man's thinking. Laws doona always stop a man from acting, either. Folks in these parts have long memories. Ye need to take care."

Janet Horne had been burned twenty years ago. Not that long ago for people with long memories. And this was the eighteenth century. Women had no rights.

Thea tried to suppress another shudder.

Chapter Fifteen

"This just arrived for you." Thea stepped inside Ian's study and handed him a sealed letter.

"I was going to bring it to ye," Cora said from behind her, "but she wouldna let me have it."

"Stop being silly," Moire, having followed Thea as well, said to Cora. "'Tis nae important who delivers a letter. What is important is who it is from." She turned to Ian. "It has nae seal, which makes it mysterious."

"Which is, I assume, why all three of ye are here?" Ian asked.

"Well, I have nae heard from my father recently," Moire said.

"And my father always needs to ken if more wounded are expected." Cora slipped a sideways glance at Thea. "So that he can prepare the surgery."

To her credit, Thea didn't respond, for which Ian was thankful. The last few days had been tense, although Callum hadn't made any further accusations and Thea had managed to stay out of his way. Still, Ian didn't need any more provocations.

He opened the missive, not particularly surprised that it was from the prince. Putting a royal—or soon-to-be-royal—seal on an envelope would only serve as an enticement for someone to open it or, worse, steal it. Ian skimmed the few paragraphs and tossed it on the desk.

"I'm to send more troops. The English have been

raiding the lands of Cameron of Lochiel and MacDonald of Keppoch, and the prince wants to reward their loyalties by pushing the Redcoats back."

"Back to where?" Moire asked. "He can't mean the border, can ye?"

"Although that would be good riddance," Cora said—and glanced at Thea again. "Anyone who is nae a Highlander should be gone."

Ian suppressed a sigh. Ever since the night he'd sent Cora back into the house, she'd held some sort of grudge toward Thea. Having her father resent Thea as well didn't help matters. He shook his head in answer to Moire's question. "Nae quite that far. The English are quartered at Fort Augustus."

"And the prince wants to attack the fort?" Thea asked.

Ian gave her a careful look before answering. He hoped she wasn't going to do another prediction about the outcome, especially with Cora in the room. Better to forge ahead with what he knew about the place. Both Cameron and MacDonald had said the fort had unsturdy walls since it was built with angled bastions at each corner, which could be weakened with a few well-placed cannon shots. They'd urged Cromartie to consider flattening it many times before. It sounded like it was finally going to happen. "It should nae be hard to take since it was nae built well to begin with."

Thea nodded. "I think you are right."

Ian narrowed his eyes slightly in warning and she, in turn, slightly widened hers. He wasn't sure if it was in understanding not to continue or whether she was mocking him by looking innocent. It was a bit irritating not to be certain and, paradoxically, he wanted to know if he were right. Which of course meant that he was beginning to believe her fantasy. He closed his eyes briefly. When he opened them again, Thea was smiling at him, looking very much like a cat who'd found the creamery door open.

She truly was going to drive him barmy.

****

If Cora hadn't been in the room, Thea would have laughed out loud at the changing expressions on Ian's face as he first gave her an appraising look, followed by what could be a "warning" before totally closing his eyes as if the problem of who she really was would go away. Not that she was foolish enough to make any "predictions" in front of Cora. She didn't need to give Callum any more fodder for his idiotic thoughts.

Still, she couldn't resist teasing Ian a bit.

"It's a shame you can't summon up the Oracle of Delphi." Thea smiled. "Maybe she could eliminate some of the uncertainty the prince faces."

Ian frowned at her, but before he could say anything, Cora spoke up.

"Who's that?" she asked. "And how could she do that?"

Thea hadn't expected an actual question, but a thought flitted through her mind. Maybe if she went into detail about the absurdity of what the ancient Greeks believed—that a woman who was basically high on some kind of hallucinogen could deliver outcomes—the girl would realize how silly her father's claims of witchcraft were, since that was even more absurd.

"Well, when I visited Athens, I heard of her. Her name was Pythia, and she was the high priestess to Apollo. His temple—one of them—was built into the wall of a mountain similar to those here in the Highlands. People would travel from far away to ask her to predict outcomes for whatever they were asking." Thea ignored Ian's deepening frown. "She sat on a gilded tripod above an opening in a cleft in the rock, inhaling the vapors and fumes that emerged." Ian was now glowering at her, but she waved a hand airily. "Pythia would then go into a trance and tell the questioner what Apollo's answer was." She pasted on a bright smile. "Quite the story, isn't it?"

Cora didn't smile back. "Ye think…someone…can make predictions about Scotland?"

"Nae, she doesna." Ian gave Thea a final admonishing look before turning to Cora. "Ye ken no one can predict the future."

Cora studied Thea a moment longer before replying. "I ken 'twould be the work of the devil."

Thea felt a chill race through her blood at those words. Her attempt at levity had certainly backfired. She should have known Cora wouldn't understand. Avoiding Ian's now-penetrating look, she shrugged in what she hoped was a nonchalant manner. "It was just a story about the ancient Greeks. Of course, *I* don't think anyone can predict the future."

Which was a completely different thing from knowing the future because she was from it. But she wasn't about to open that topic.

****

Ian breathed a sigh of relief as he watched the last of the troops he'd been training disappear over the ridge on their march toward Inverness to join Cromartie. With no men practicing in the courtyard, it meant no one was going to get injured, which, in turn, meant the surgery would be empty. And that meant he wouldn't have to worry about Thea and Callum clashing anytime soon.

"It won't be long before injured men begin to return," Thea said as if reading his mind.

Another thought that left him vaguely uneasy. Standing beside him, her silvery-blue eyes catching the morning light and with her hair, loosened from the wind that whistled around the corner of the castle, floating around her face like pale silk, she looked ethereal. Fae. But she couldn't possibly know his thoughts. He wasn't even going to consider that. It was bad enough he was losing his mind over the idea of traveling through time. He glanced around the now-empty barracks. "I hope that's nae another one of your predictions."

She smiled. "No. Just a logical conclusion to senseless battles in a senseless war."

He drew his brows together. "Ye have to stop talking like that, even if ye doona favor the Jacobites."

"I don't favor either side," she answered. "Shedding blood is not necessary."

He felt his jaw set. "It is, if we're going to have a Stuart king rule Scotland."

She tilted her head to gaze up at him. "So you believe in the divine right of kings? Isn't that what caused Charles I to lose his head?"

"Charles was a tyrant, by all accounts," Ian replied, "and his son was eventually restored to the throne, which just shows that Cromwell's Commonwealth couldn't keep a Stuart off the throne."

"All that changed when neither Mary or Anne bore any children." Thea shook her head. "Your present 'prince' was raised in Rome and Paris. He never even set foot in Scotland before last year."

"It doesna matter. He is a Stuart."

"Maybe by blood, but does that make him a Scot?"

Ian frowned again. "What do ye mean by that?"

"I mean, in here." Thea placed a hand across her heart.

The innocuous gesture immediately drew his attention to the full breasts which rested under her fingers. Even though her bodice was modest with a high neckline, there was no hiding those luscious mounds. He forced himself to lift his gaze only to find her watching him intently much like a hunting dog might, alert to its prey. Did she know the effect she had on him? Ever since she'd lain on top of him at Hogmanay he'd felt desire. A desire he'd tried to squelch even though the second kiss they'd shared hadn't helped at all. Still. He thought he was better at masking his feelings. He gave himself a mental shake. "What do ye mean by that?" he repeated.

"I mean, just because Stuart blood is running through Charles's veins, does that mean he know what it means to be a Scot? Does he understand what it means to be part of this land? Its harshness? Its isolation? Its mountains and glens? Its rugged, natural beauty?"

"Ye describe Scotland well."

"I love this country. But does Charles? He's never lived here."

"He will learn to love it."

Thea shrugged. "I suppose it's possible, but he was raised in cities."

"We have Edinburgh and Glasgow, lass."

"Hmmm. But I wonder if Charles came here because he wants to be a prince and he has Stuart blood in his veins."

"'Tis the Stuart blood that matters."

Thea considered. "Well, if that's true, there's another one with Stuart blood that would most likely want to become king as well."

Ian widened his eyes. "There's another Stuart who wants to lay claim to the throne?"

She nodded. "But you don't have to worry. He lives in the twenty-first century."

Ian groaned. He thought they'd been having a more or less rational discussion. And now they weren't. Again.

Chapter Sixteen

"Ye ken Ian doesna agree when ye say ye doona think fighting for the Cause is necessary?" Moire asked the next day when they were alone in the solar.

"I do know." It would be hard for Thea not to get that point, especially since after their argument, Ian had talked about the importance of the Stuart dynasty at dinner last night and she had stupidly—hindsight was humiliating—pressed her point for stopping bloodshed. It had gotten her stares, some scrutinizing. Not to mention a penetrating warning look from Ian himself. "I understand that Scotland wants its independence. I don't blame Scots for not wanting to be under the control of the English either."

"Then why do ye think we should stop fighting?"

Thea shook her head. "What I'm saying is it would be better to meet at a negotiating table to work matters out."

"'Twould be surrender."

"You sound like Ian now." Thea frowned. "Are you a staunch supporter of the prince, then? Even though you own father is on the government side?"

"I try nae to think about it," Moire said.

"That's not really an answer, though."

Moire lifted both hands. "What can I do? 'Tis nae just my uncle and father who are on opposite sides."

"You are right about that. Your General Murray is

about to attack his own brother at their clan seat."

"How do ye ken that?"

Blast it. Her mouth had gotten her into trouble again. For a moment, Thea fervently wished she knew how she'd travelled back in time so she could undo the last few minutes. "You told me earlier that General Murray's brother James was pro-English. Since the Jacobites have destroyed both Fort George and now Fort Augustus, it would make sense to claim Blair Castle because of its proximity." She lifted one shoulder in what she hoped was a nonchalant shrug. "It's just an educated guess on my part."

Moire was silent, studying her. After what seemed like agonizingly long minutes had passed, she finally spoke.

"It seems to me that ye have made a number of educated guesses about this war. 'Tis unusual for a woman to ken military strategies."

"Well, I…have studied history. It tends to repeat itself." Even to her own ears, that sounded lame. "I mean, right now on the Continent, the war for Austrian succession is taking place. When Maria Theresa Habsburg's father died, Saxony, Bavaria, and France all repudiated her claim to be Holy Roman Empress. Frederick of Prussia is her worst rival. What's happening in Scotland can mirror what's happening in Prussia…especially since King George is Frederick's uncle," she added. 'Who knows what contact they have?"

Moire stayed silent for another long moment. "That may verra well be, but ye seem to ken—nae just think— that we will lose our Cause." She tilted her head as if she were studying an unusual specimen. "Why is that?"

Thea was at a loss for words. What excuse could she make? A thought struck her like one of the capers thrown at the Highland Games. Should she make an excuse? Maybe she should tell Moire the truth. In the time she'd been at Kilcoy, they'd become friends. She knew she could trust her. There wouldn't be any speculation about witches or devils. As mad as the truth might sound initially, Moire was inquisitive and creative. If Thea could convince her where she came from, maybe she'd have an ally in convincing Ian too. Something needed to be done to make him believe her before it was too late. She took a deep breath.

"It's true that I'm not simply making educated guesses about the Cause. I'm definitely not a fortune teller or anything like that, but I know what's going to happen in the future."

Moire studied her again, this time with a look of curiosity. "How?"

"How do I know?" When she nodded, Thea took another deep breath. "I know because I am from the future. The twenty-first century, to be exact."

Moire laughed, then shook her head. "'Tis impossible."

Thea sighed. "That's what Ian keeps saying too."

Her eyes widened. "Ye have told Ian this?"

"Yes. Right after we met at Hogmanay." She wasn't going to say exactly how they met, although she could still recall—vividly—straddling his hard, muscular body and—even more vividly—the feel of his mouth on hers and the sensation of his kisses. "He asked where I was from and I told him."

"Ye told him ye were from the future?"

"Originally, I told him I was from Texas—"

"Where?"

Thea waved a hand. "Never mind. It's a long story about the Colonies revolting and the formation of the United States of America…south of where Nova Scotia is, but that's not important right now." She put a hand briefly on Moire's shoulder. "What is important is that you at least consider what I'm saying is true. I am from the future."

Moire knit her brows. "I doona understand how that could happen."

"Neither do I." Thea grimaced. "I've gone over it a thousand times."

"But how….?" Moire let her voice trail off.

Thea sighed again. "I was with my friends—in the twenty-first century—celebrating Hogmanay and I saw Ian fall down—"

"Here? In Inverness?"

"Yes. Well, no. I mean it was in Inverness, but…there. In my time."

"Go on."

It was a good sign that Moire appeared at least willing to listen. "I was worried that he might have hurt himself, since he didn't move. I went over and leaned down to check on him. I suddenly felt like I was falling…and the next thing I knew when I opened my eyes was that I was in a different century." Better to leave out the part of his grabbing her hand and how intent his gaze had been. She could still feel the instant tingle of his touch just before she drifted into nothingness. "And here I am. I have no idea what happened and I don't know how to go back. However, I do know what is going to happen with the Cause." She paused. "The Jacobites are going to get massacred at Culloden unless I can put a stop to it."

"Culloden? Why would they be there? 'Tis a boggy moor."

"Because the prince wants to surprise Cumberland."

"The duke?" Moire's forehead wrinkled. "Why would he go to Culloden?"

"It's complicated." Thea gave Moire an intense look. "It might be able to be avoided if I can just get Ian to listen to me."

"Ye might have better luck talking to a rock."

Thea would have laughed if the situation weren't so serious. "I think it would help if you told him that you believed me."

"But I doona ken if I do." Moire held up her hands. "Ye have to admit, 'tis a wee bit barmy-sounding."

"It's more than a wee bit," Thea admitted. "I wouldn't believe it either, except I know it happened." She looked at Moire pensively. "Maybe if I can tell you what is going to happen at Blair Castle—and it turns out to be true—you'll believe me?"

Moire inhaled. "I might."

"Okay, then." Thea hoped she could remember all the facts. Vi, being a history professor, had talked incessantly about the events leading up to Culloden as they planned their trip to Scotland. "The Jacobites will take the outposts to Blair Castle by surprise and capture English soldiers. General Murray will then lay siege to the castle, even though it is his family seat. He'll even fire at it from close range. The baronet who's in command will refuse to surrender. He'll try to get a messenger through the lines and ask for reinforcement, but the rider will be stopped. The prince will recall General Murray to Inverness since Cumberland is enlarging his army at Aberdeen."

"You think Cumberland is gathering more troops? Ian thinks King George sent him up here mainly for bluster to scare the prince."

Thea shook her head. "This isn't saber-rattling. Cumberland will attack." She paused once more. "And the Jacobites will lose."

****

They were still at the table the next morning breaking their fast when a messenger arrived from Ardsheal. Ian was tempted to wait until everyone had finished eating so he could open the missive privately, but several pairs of eyes were trained on him expectantly. He sighed, put down his spoon, and broke the seal.

"Cumberland appears to be gathering more soldiers at Aberdeen," he said.

Moire made a gasping sound and looked at Thea who, if he wasn't imagining things, nodded ever so slightly. What were they communicating to each other? And Moire had gone pale, which was unusual too.

Evidently, Cora caught the interchange also since she narrowed her eyes at Thea and then looked at Moire. "What's wrong?"

Moire shook her head. "Nothing."

Not to be deterred, Cora pressed on. "Ye sounded like ye were taking your last breath."

"I…just got something stuck in my throat." Moire reached for her goblet and took a sip. "There. Much better."

Cora still looked dubious, although she remained silent, but now Callum was looking at Moire as well. "Ye do look a wee bit peaked."

"It's nothing," Moire said again and glanced briefly

at Thea before shaking her head once more. "I…I'm fine."

Color was coming back to her cheeks, Ian noted with relief and then covertly watched Thea. A small smile curled her lips and she looked extremely pleased with herself. But for what?

Moire took another sip and set her cup down. "Does Ardsheal say where General Murray is?"

A startled expression crossed Thea's face. For a moment, she sat rigid as a statue before assuming a more relaxed mode. She had stopped smiling and was watching Moire intently. Was another message being passed? Ian frowned and turned back to Moire.

"Ardsheal doesn't mention Murray. Why do ye ask?"

"I…I was just wondering." Moire glanced at Thea again. "If Cumberland is gathering men, I thought maybe…General Murray might want to…find out if any of his brother's soldiers will be going to Aberdeen to join the duke."

The complacent smile was back on Thea's face. Something was definitely going on between the two women. But what?

****

Thea felt like every nerve ending was standing at attention. The fact that the messenger had arrived this morning, right after she'd told Moire it was going to happen, couldn't have been better timing and coincided perfectly with what she'd said. But then she'd nearly gone into cardiac arrest when Moire asked about General Murray. Blair Castle had not yet been under attack and, if Moire said too much in front of Callum and Cora, it would not bode well, especially if Ian then started asking questions. He already had a suspicious look in his eyes.

"That's a good question," she said, "and it makes me wonder if perhaps the prince will be bringing back the men he sent to Fort Augustus."

Ian's expression turned wary. He was probably afraid she was going to blurt out another prediction, which she was sorely tempted to do since she knew the men would be returning, but with Callum and Cora still at the table she wasn't going to take a chance.

"I imagine they'll come back once the Redcoats have been driven out and MacDonald and Cameron are assured their lands are no longer in danger of being raided," Ian replied. He glanced at the paper again. "Ardsheal just wants us to be aware what's happening."

Moire nodded. "I suppose there's no need for concern right now. My father always says there's no advantage to marching through snow to attack." She gave Thea a quick glance before turning back to Ian. "Cumberland might attack in the spring, though."

Thea tried to keep her face impassive, but she really wanted to shout for joy. Did the fact that Moire brought up the idea of what might possibly happen—after she'd told her what would happen—mean her friend was beginning to believe her?

Chapter Seventeen

"Do the generals really think it wise to try taking Fort William?" Thea asked Ian a few days later after she'd brought the latest message to him.

"'Tis nae the generals. 'Tis the prince who wants to proceed." Ian put the letter down on the desk. "He feels they had success in destroying Forts George and Augustus." He eyed her speculatively. "Why do ye nae think they can take Fort William too?"

Thea felt a spark of hope that he'd asked. Did that mean he was beginning to believe that maybe she did know what the future held?

"Well, it's better situated and better fortified than the other two, isn't it?"

"Aye. 'Tis why neither General Murray nor Colonel Stapleton think it wise to attack."

"They cannot persuade the prince?"

Ian sighed. "Prince Charles is feeling pressure from Cameron and MacDonald, who insist their lands are still being raided."

"Maybe if MacDonald and Cameron were told that Cumberland is amassing troops and the Jacobite army might need to be back here, they'd understand?"

"I gave that information to the messenger to relay." Ian grimaced. "It would be a lot faster to bring the men and artillery back if we had a direct waterway between Fort Augustus and Fort William like we have from

Inverness to Augustus via Loch Ness." He shook his head. "'Tis nae use to fantasize, though. It canna happen."

"It's not a farfetched idea. The Greeks did it with the Isthmus Canal. They cut through the isthmus of Corinth to link the Ionian Sea to the Aegean." She smiled. "Although it did take them twenty-five hundred years to complete."

"Twenty-five *hundred* years?" Ian raised a brow, then laughed and leaned back in his chair. "I could use an entertaining story right now to take my mind off this, so tell me."

"Well." She ignored the fact that he thought this was funny. "It all began around the seventh century BCE when Periander, one of the Seven Sages and the ruler of Corinth, wanted to connect the Ionian and Aegean seas surrounding the isthmus. Pythia—you remember, the Oracle of Delphi?—proclaimed such a thing would anger the gods. although that didn't stop the Spartans from trying in the sixth century or the Macedonians in the third. The Romans—including Julius Caesar and Nero—tried three times, and each time the leader met death." Thea gave Ian an inquiring look to know if he wanted her to go on and he gave her a nod, looking suitably impressed. She paused since this was where it was going to get tricky. Taking a deep breath, she rushed to finish. "The canal was finally navigable in 1893, but it was damaged by an earthquake in 1928 and a fire in 1933. However, it still exists." She stilled and folded her hands in her lap.

Ian simply stared at her. For what seemed like a century in itself, he said nothing. Then he shook his head.

"Just when I think ye are talking sensibly, ye start

talking about something that makes nae sense at all."

"It does make sense," she answered, "because it happened."

He shook his head again, but before he could respond, she went on. "And let me tell you also that a canal will happen here. In Scotland. And exactly where you would like it to be."

"'Tis nonsense."

"It's not. It will be called the Caledonian Canal—or Neptune's Ladder—and will connect Inverness to Fort William via a system of twenty-nine locks. It won't be built, though, until the early 1800s—

"Stop talking such nonsense, lass!"

Thea glared at him, trying to ignore the fact that she was irresistibly attracted to this obstinate creature. Sometimes she thought if she just grabbed him and kissed him senseless, maybe she could penetrate that thick skull of his. Right now, she was so frustrated at his refusal to even consider the possibility that she spoke the truth that she wanted to stomp her foot like a child. Instead, she got up and walked to the door. Before she left, she turned around.

"Fort William will not fall. Maybe you'll believe me when you find out that I'm right."

And with that, she left him staring after her.

****

Ian started to shake his head at her departure and then stopped himself. He didn't need to rattle his brains any more than they already were. He'd never met a more confusing woman, though. One minute she was talking rationally or telling a mythical story, and then she would launch into something about the future that was completely fabricated.

Or was it fabricated? She'd been right about a number of things. Was that just coincidence? Or—Lord, help him because he may have already gone completely mad himself—was it possible that she was right? Could she be from the future?

****

When the next message arrived, this one from Cromartie, Ian went to the door himself, although when he turned around, Thea, Moire, and Cora all stood expectantly awaiting him in the foyer. For a moment he considered carrying the sealed letter to his study and shutting the door firmly, but the women would probably not be daunted at that. Moiré, especially, thought nothing of barging in unannounced, and Thea would not be far behind. Cora would eventually know what the missive contained because he would have to share it with her father. He might as well handle the situation now.

"Follow me," he said.

Once they were all seated, he broke the seal. The first paragraph regarded Fort William. "Our troops have blockaded the loch at Corran Narrows," he said, "so the English won't be getting supplies. Fort William is under siege." He glanced at Thea, but she just smiled serenely. He frowned and returned to the letter and then his brow cleared.

"Good news?" Moire asked.

"Aye. Verra good. Lieutenant General Drummond has confiscated not only seven hundred English weapons, but captured over three hundred of Loudoun's refugee soldiers."

"Where?" Thea asked.

"Meikle's ferry near Dornoch." He smirked a bit. At least, this wasn't an event that Thea had predicted.

"Apparently, Loudoun got word that they would be attacked and he thought it would come from across the firth at River Shin since that was the most logical approach—"

"Only that isn't what the Jacobites did, was it?" Thea asked.

Ian drew his brows together. Was she going to claim she knew about this episode too? She hadn't mentioned it before. Still, he sent her a warning glance. She didn't need to be making any comment in front of Cora. Thea just widened her eyes innocently, though. Exasperating woman. She kept him on edge, a feeling he was not familiar with. What he was familiar with, though, was the randy reaction his manhood made whenever he was in her presence. He wondered how hard she would slap him if he satiated his desire by kissing her senseless. He gritted his teeth and pushed the thought from his mind.

"No. About five hundred men from Clan Fraser and another three hundred from Clan MacGregor came on shore at the ferry landing, instead, and marched to Skibo Castle. Unfortunately, Loudoun wasn't there, but the guard retreated and, when Cromartie arrived with reinforcements, the remaining soldiers surrendered."

"How many got away?" Thea asked.

Ian glanced at the letter again. "Cromartie isn't sure, but he thinks about nine hundred." He put the letter down. "They're probably headed for Skye, which would be a safe haven to regroup."

Thea gave him a long look, one that he couldn't interpret but made him uneasy. He hoped she wasn't going to blurt out another prediction. He shook his head slightly at her. She acknowledged that with a slight nod.

"I suspect Skye will make a good getaway," she

said.

The remark sounded innocuous enough, but the hair at his nape began to rise. Did she mean something else?

****

Thea had wanted to tell him that if she couldn't stop the battle at Culloden from happening, Bonnie Prince Charlie would be taking that escape route too, after the massacre. But with Cora in the room, it would have to wait. Another thought struck her. Maybe the prince wouldn't have to escape—or maybe he'd escape much earlier—if the Jacobites could be stopped where they were right now and the war could end.

"If those thousand men that escaped from Dornoch actually head for Skye, wouldn't that put the prince in a dangerous position?" she asked.

Ian gave her a thoughtful look before answering. He was probably wondering where she was going with this. She wanted to tell him not to worry that she was going to make another prediction because this time she didn't know. She didn't remember Vi saying anything about government soldiers on Skye. But it wouldn't be relevant if the course of history changed.

"How so?" he finally asked.

"Well, some of the soldiers at Fort Augustus must have escaped, and Fort William hasn't been taken—"

"Yet," he said.

"Yet," she conceded since she didn't want to contradict him in front of Cora. "That means there are English soldiers to the west of him as well as to the northwest, not to mention government soldiers south in England—"

"What is your point?" Cora interrupted. "We ken that."

Thea ignored the rude tone and smiled pleasantly. "The point is that the prince may find himself surrounded by Redcoats, not to mention Scots who are loyal to the government." She turned to Ian. "How many men does the prince have with him?"

Ian frowned. "I am nae sure. About four hundred, I think."

"They're outnumbered, then," Moire said.

"And they left the heavy artillery here." It wasn't a question, since Thea had seen the cannons and other equipment lodged behind the barracks. She'd overheard talk that, with the success of destroying the other two forts, the Jacobites wanted the element of surprise at Fort William and, since the roads were not good, the artillery would just slow them down. Which meant they only had personal weapons. She was getting more hopeful by the minute that this war could be finished soon. Not that she could say that.

"Are ye saying the prince will be captured?" Cora narrowed her eyes. "Is that what ye are wanting?"

"Of course 'tis nae what Thea wants," Ian said quickly before she could answer. "Besides, we doona have to worry, with Cromartie and Murray nearby to join the prince."

"Didn't you say that Cromartie was pursuing the refugees from Fort George and Augustus?" Thea said. "He might not get word in time to rendezvous."

Moire glanced at Thea. "The same might go for General Murray."

Thea didn't acknowledge the comment, although she was glad that Moire seemed to remember—and maybe accept?—what she had said about the general.

"Well, the prince will nae surrender. He is a Stuart."

Cora smiled at Ian and reached over to put a hand on his arm. "Just like ye, and ye would nae ever give up on Scotland, either."

"Nae, I willna."

He reached for the letter, dislodging Cora's hand. Thea saw the girl's mouth tighten as she tossed a sullen glance at him. She also saw the look of determination on Ian's face and inwardly sighed. There was no point in even suggesting to Ian that this might be good time for the prince to try negotiation.

Their discussion was interrupted by Mrs. Moffat.

"I'm sorry to bother ye, but a load of lumber was just delivered from Inverness. The driver said news was all over town that General Murray has laid siege to Blair Castle and is planning to fire on it if his brother willna surrender."

Moire shot another look at Thea, and this time she nodded discreetly, although she wanted to break into a wide grin.

Her prediction had come true. She hoped now Moire would believe her and become her ally.

Stubborn as Ian Stuart was, she was going to need all the help she could get.

Chapter Eighteen

"Ye ken I could just nudge this pony to a gallop and be home in a thrice," Moire said as she, Thea, and Ian sat atop the ridge looking down at Fortrose and the vast Moray Firth beyond. "Then ye wouldna have a hostage any longer."

Ian gave her an annoyed look. "For the thousandth time, Moire, ye are nae a hostage, and ye ken it."

Moire wrinkled her nose at him. "So ye say."

Thea smiled, hoping to ease the tension she sensed building in him. "I think she's teasing you, Ian."

"I doona have much humor these days," he replied with a frown.

"Ye can say that again." Moire mimicked his frown. "Ye've been a real grouch the past few days."

"I have reason," he answered and gestured to the sea. "The French ship is late."

Thea chewed her lip, wondering how she could tell him *Le Prince Charles*—originally the *HMS Hazard* before being stolen by the Jacobites and sailed to Dunkirk to be renamed by the French king, then supplied and supposed to be setting sail for Scotland once more—wouldn't be returning.

Ian looked at her, his attention abruptly focusing on her mouth. She stopped her nibbling. For a moment, something dark flickered in his wolf-colored eyes, and then it was gone. Oddly enough, the flicker made her tummy flutter.

"Did ye wish to say something?" he asked cautiously.

"Um…yes." Thea refocused and swallowed hard. "The ship you're waiting for won't be docking here."

Ian lifted his brows and tilted his head slightly in the direction of Moire, obviously cautioning Thea to say no more.

"Ye doona have to warn her," Moire said with a wave of her hand. "Thea's already told me she's from the future."

Ian looked so startled Thea was afraid he might fall off his horse. Relief swept over Thea that Moire had chosen to believe her. Half the battle was won. Now to convince the other half, who was muttering something under his breath that she was sure was a Gaelic curse.

"What was that? I couldn't quite make out what ye said." She gave him a mischievous smile.

He scowled back. "Are ye daft, lass?"

"I think ye are the one who's daft, Ian," Moire said. "Everything Thea's said has come to pass."

He stared at her. "Ye canna believe someone is from the future."

Moire shrugged. "I doona understand it, but I'm nay questioning it, either. Thea's been right. Mayhap ye should listen to her."

He looked dumbfounded. Thea felt a giggle rising at the fact that he was clearly speechless for once, but she suppressed it. Better press her advantage while he was still quiet. "Do you want to hear the rest?"

The question seemed to bring him out of his stupor. His expression changed to resigned. "Why nae? Go on with it, then."

"The ship's been captured. Well, not yet, but it will be. I'm not sure exactly when. Soon, I mean." Thea silently chastised herself for sounding like a garbled nincompoop. She took a deep breath. "If I recall correctly, the ship was spotted by the English as it was sailing past Aberdeen. One of the captains recognized it as being the former *Hazard* and gave chase. The Scottish captain put into the Kyle of Tongue, hoping the bigger ship would flounder—"

"The Kyle of Tongue? 'Tis nae that far from here," Ian said, turning his horse around. "I will go back to the castle and get help. We can be there in—"

"Wait," Thea called and he reined in. "You are—or will be—too late. Some of Loudoun's refugees who did not flee attacked the ship in the shallow water. The supplies were taken." She hesitated, then added, "And so were over a hundred and fifty men."

Ian's eyes widened. "Captured?"

"I'm afraid so." Thea took another deep breath. "You should be getting the news any day now."

****

The news arrived within forty-eight hours. Not only had the ship been taken, but thirteen thousand pounds in gold as well as supplies, arms, and other weapons King Louis had provided in support of the Cause were now in the hands of the English. As were the entire crew of *Le Prince Charles*.

Ian looked at the man who'd delivered the message. "Ye are sure of this?"

The man nodded miserably. "Aye. One of the crew managed to escape and brought the news himself to the prince."

"Any idea of where the English would take the

hostages?"

"We canna be sure, but with both Fort George and Fort Augustus destroyed, Cromartie thinks they may be heading toward Dunrobin Castle in Sutherland. The English still hold it."

"That would make sense," Ian said. "Is there any chance of intercepting them before they reach it?"

The man shook his head. "We got the news too late. By the time the sailor reached us, the Redcoats had several days' lead. The prince did send out scouts, though."

"And they found nae trace?"

"Nae. The road was clear. 'Tis likely the prisoners are behind the castle walls."

"Do ye ken what the prince plans to do about this?"

"Aye. Cromartie is planning to lay siege to the castle." The man offered a slight smile. "In exchange for the hostages, he'll let the castle stand."

A corner of Ian's mouth lifted too. "I doubt the Redcoats will truly appreciate that gesture." Which they should, since the Jacobites were using a lesson well learned from Robert the Bruce to leave no castle or fort standing to be re-taken by the enemy.

"Is there anything the prince or Ardsheal want me to do?"

"Just gather more troops." The man stood to leave. "I need to ride on to alert the Frasers and Farquarsons, since some of their clansmen were among the crew."

Ian sat at his desk after the man left, staring at the closed door yet not seeing it. His mind turned to previous discussions he'd had with Thea. Moire had been correct…everything Thea had "predicted" had come to pass. There wasn't any way even the generals could have known the outcome of those events. And yet each and every one had turned out exactly as she said.

Ian rubbed his temple, willing the oncoming headache to go away. He tried to think. Thea had appeared suddenly at Hogmanay, alone and without funds or even extra clothing. Her "friends" had been nowhere to be found. Buildings she described in Inverness were not there. Malcolm Ross didn't recognize her and said he'd never heard of her…

There was no reasonable, logical explanation for any of it. Lord knew he had tried to figure it out and was in the process of driving himself mad. There was only one impossible-to-believe option. Slowly, he realized it was one he'd have to accept, whether it was barmy or not.

Athena Ross was from the future.

Chapter Nineteen

"You believe me?" Thea asked, not quite sure she wasn't imagining what Ian had just said. "You actually, really, truly believe me?"

Ian glanced at the study door as if he needed reassuring that it was closed before he looked back at her. "Aye. I believe ye are from…" He hesitated, then nodded. "I believe ye are from the future."

Thea felt giddy. She wanted nothing more than to jump up, throw her arms around Ian, and shower kisses on him, but given that his facial expression looked carved in stone and how rigidly still he sat, she was pretty sure he was using the desk between them as a barrier, maybe still trying to convince himself that he had come to a sane conclusion.

"What convinced you? Was it what Moire said?"

"Partly. Hearing someone else say she believed it was possible that ye were from the future made it not seem quite so…impossible. Then the messenger confirmed what ye said about the French ship," Ian replied. "And now, our army called off the siege at Fort William and returned to Inverness…just like ye said it would."

Thea nodded. "Now all we have to do is convince the prince and the generals not to fight at Culloden."

Ian frowned. "Ye are sure the battle will take place on Drummossie Moor?"

"I am. Not only do history books describe the massacre in detail, but in my century, there is a visitor center with a three-dimensional—"

"What's that?"

"It's…it's like a diagram with realistic soldiers and buildings set on a big table. Visitors can see what the battlefield looked like and listen to an audio—"

"An audio? What's that?"

"An audio is a taped recording…" She held up her hand before he could ask what a taped recording was. "It's someone 'talking' but not really in person." She sighed in frustration. "It's hard to explain. I wish you could just go to the twenty-first century and experience it for yourself."

He was quiet for a moment. "I think I would like that." He gave her a thoughtful look. "Do ye think I could travel to your time?"

"I wish I could make it happen, but I don't even know how *I* got *here*," Thea answered, "but it might help for you to know there is actually a shrine—a cairn—that serves as a monument on the battlefield. You can also walk around and read the clan names on the mass grave markers."

"There are that many?"

"Clans MacGillivray, MacLean, MacDonald, Mackintosh, Fraser, Cameron—to name just a few." She paused. "Stuart of Appin is there as well."

"My people," he said softly.

"I'm sorry to be the bearer of this news, but now you can see why it's imperative that we change the prince's mind."

Ian hesitated. "Does the prince survive?"

Thea nodded. "He escapes to Skye and then to the

Continent, where he will live out his life in Rome." She tilted her head to study Ian. "For the record, there is a man in my time who claims to be a descendant of the prince."

"He is king of Scotland?"

"No. Unfortunately, Scotland is still ruled by Britain."

Ian stared at her and then sighed. "So that's why ye think our Cause is in vain."

"Yes. Which is why it's imperative to keep the battle at Culloden from happening. Someone has to convince the prince."

"I'm nae sure 'tis possible. Word came from Murray that the prince is feeling victorious and looks forward to meeting Cumberland."

Thea wanted to say the prince was a fool, but that was neither here nor there and would only irritate Ian, which she couldn't afford to do right now. "I understand that, but I think he's making the same mistake that will be made in the Peloponnese peninsula. Remember what I told you?"

"Aye, but that doesna mean Prince Charlie will lose his fight."

"My point is that the *current* British Empire—like the Ottomans—is too powerful to overcome at the present time."

Ian frowned. "David beat Goliath, didna he?"

Thea sighed. "This isn't a Biblical analogy, Ian. I would love to see Scotland be victorious and claim independence. But this isn't the time. If the battle at Culloden occurs, you will lose. Not only will thousands of men die, but you'll be forbidden to own weapons or wear tartan." She rose. "Scotland will lose her whole way of life."

****

"Thea! Thea! Come quickly!" Moire burst into the solar where Thea sat by a window, carefully stitching a tear to the sleeve of a bodice. She tossed the garment down and leapt up.

"What is it? What's wrong?"

"Come!" Moire grabbed Thea's hand and pulled her toward the door. "Liam Munro—a crofter—brought his son Darach to the surgery. A boar wounded him and he's bleeding badly."

"Is Callum not there?" Thea asked as they hurried down the stairs.

"Nae. Since the army returned, he went into Inverness this morning to purchase more supplies."

"Who's tending the boy?" Thea asked as they reached the pantry off the kitchen where she kept her supplies.

"Ian's there. He's trying to hold the wound closed, but it's bleeding a lot."

"All right." Thea hurriedly gathered what she needed and raced outside, Moire running behind her. Even though the surgery had a number of windows to allow light in, it still took a moment for her eyes to adjust after the sun shining on new snow. The unconscious youth lying on the surgery table looked to be just past puberty. Ian leaned over him, both blood-covered hands on his abdomen, while a distraught man paced back and forth beside him, alternately cursing and praying.

Cora came out of the backroom carrying bandages. "What are ye doing here? I am helping Ian."

"I need Thea," Ian said. "I canna stop the blood by myself. Hurry, lass!"

Thea turned to the work table, quickly shaking dried hemlock leaves onto a dried poultice dressing which she then dipped in the water basin and rushed over to Ian. An involuntary gasp escaped her lips when she reached him.

There was an actual hole in the boy's stomach from where one of the tusks must have gored him. Though it wasn't wide, it was deep and she was afraid the intestines might have been ripped apart. There was nothing she could do about that right now. Stopping the bleeding was the first priority.

"Press down on my hands," she told Ian as she slipped the poultice under his. "Hard."

"I doona want to hurt ye."

"Never mind that. We need to apply enough pressure to keep more blood from spilling. It'll help the hemlock get into the wound faster too."

"Hemlock?" Cora asked. "My father says 'tis poison."

"It is if you eat it," Thea replied, "but it works for wounds."

Liam stopped pacing. "Are ye sure? Have ye done this before?"

"No, but at the moment I don't have any other choice." Thea tried not to grimace at the pain shooting through her fingers from Ian's hands bearing down. She didn't dare ask him to lessen his hold. The boy couldn't afford to lose much more blood.

Liam began his pacing again. After what seemed like half an eternity, the bleeding slowed to a trickle and then finally stopped. "Bring the bandages," she said to Cora.

The girl sidled up to Ian. "What do ye wish for me to do?"

"Whatever Thea tells ye to do."

Cora's expression turned pouty and she thrust the bandages at Thea. "Here, then."

Thankfully, Thea managed to catch them since she had almost no feeling left in her fingers. Not that she was going to admit to that. The important thing was that the bleeding had stopped, the poultice helping to plug the wound. She started to lay the bandage across the boy's stomach when Ian's hand stayed her.

"I will bandage him."

Thea gave him a quizzical look and then felt her cheeks warm as she realized that the boy was probably naked under the sheet that had partially covered him. "Of course. I'll just go and wash up." She turned away.

"Thank God the bleeding's stopped." Liam said to Ian as he approached the table. "I should never have taken Dorach hunting with me, but my prayers have been answered now."

Thea heard his comments, but she didn't turn around. The bleeding had been halted, but depending on what other injury the boy had sustained, Liam's prayers may very well not have been answered.

****

"Where are ye going?"

Thea turned from the kitchen door that led outside to face Ian. "I thought to go check on Darach this morning."

"'Tis best if ye doona."

She frowned. "Why not?"

"Callum is still in a bit of a temper."

"*An diabhal galsh am fireannach*," she muttered, one of the Gaelic curses she'd heard Ian use.

His eyebrows rose in surprise. "What did ye say?"

"You heard me. *The devil take the man.*"

Ian grinned. "I'm nae sure the devil would want him."

"Probably true." When Callum had returned from Inverness last night, instead of being thankful she'd been available to help Darach, he'd been angry to find out she'd used his surgery. And that his equipment wasn't in exact order as he'd left it. But his ranting had gotten even worse when he found the poultice—which he wasn't supposed to remove—had contained hemlock leaves. He'd nearly gone ballistic, claiming she was trying to poison the lad. Ian had finally told him he'd not listen to another word. That he'd been there and the poultice had stopped the bleeding. Callum had sullenly retreated to his supply room, slamming the door shut. She sighed.

"I suppose you're right. I wouldn't want to upset Darach by having a shouting match in front of him. Maybe I could talk to Liam, though, and see how the boy fared?"

"Ye'll have to wait for him to return. I convinced him to go home last night since his wife didn't know what had happened and she'd be worried if neither one of them returned."

"I hadn't thought of that. Well, then maybe you can go out there and find out?"

Ian nodded and reached for the door, only to have it fly open, nearly hitting him in the face.

A furious Callum stood there, his face so red it was nearly purple with rage. "Darach is dead." He attempted to step inside, but Ian blocked him. He glared at him and pointed a finger at Thea. "She's a witch. She murdered the lad with her poison!"

****

171

The next few days passed in a blur for Thea. She would never forget the sounds of Liam's roar or his wife's keening when they found out their son had died. She'd wanted to go out and talk to them, to explain that the boar had probably pierced Darach's intestines and he'd probably bled to death internally, but Ian wouldn't let her. Instead, he'd locked her in an upstairs room.

In which she was still a prisoner. Ian had denied that she was, telling her it was for her own safety. That the guard posted outside her door was for her protection. But, like Moire, she wasn't free to leave. She began to pace. Again.

At least she wasn't in a dungeon—she'd discovered that Kilcoy did have one—or the attic, which is where a lot of women got banished to. The room was comfortable with a featherbed, table and chairs, and a small brazier. Hot food was brought at mealtimes and Moire was allowed to visit. Ian had reiterated that it was for Thea's own good if Callum and Liam thought he'd locked her up until they could think rationally. Tempers needed to cool. Moire had even agreed, more or less, with him, pointing out that some people still believed in witches and that the old healer had to abandon her cottage in the woods because of threats. Just because witch-burning was banned didn't mean it couldn't happen.

Thea sank down on the bed. Moire was right. Mob mentality, whether concerning eighteenth-century witches or the rioting that took place for various reasons in the twenty-first century, was not easily controlled. And Ian was one man. He couldn't hold off an angry crowd.

But when would it end? What was her future—she felt a hysterical giggle bubble up at the pun and

squelched it—what was her *future* to be?
****

It was on the first day of April—which would be April Fool's Day in her time, and Thea hoped the date wasn't some kind of ironic twist—that Ian finally felt things had calmed down enough for her to no longer be confined. Callum had ceased his grumbling, and Liam and his wife hadn't been seen, apparently quietly grieving at their crofter cottage.

Still, Thea was surprised when Cora approached her in the garden where she'd gone to enjoy fresh air on her first day out of "captivity." It had snowed the night before, leaving the ground a pristine white under the winter sun, making her think of fresh starts. Cora was smiling as she came toward her, so maybe it would be a fresh start with the girl as well.

"Do ye mind if I have a word with ye?" she asked.

"Of course not," Thea replied, trying to sound as neutral as possible. "What's on your mind?"

"Well…" Cora looked down and shuffled her feet, then looked up. "I would like to apologize for my father. He accused ye of witchcraft."

Thea tried to hide her surprise. Maybe Cora—since she was younger than the folks who'd actually participated in previous witch hunts—really thought her father had gone overboard. "Thank you. Did you talk to him about it?"

"Aye. We had a long talk. 'Twas good to get the air cleared." She looked down again, then raised her gaze. "I should apologize as well. I have nae been very friendly."

It was a good thing there wasn't much of a breeze or Thea might have been blown over like a feather. Cora was sorry for her rude behavior? Thea wondered if perhaps Ian had spoken with Cora too, while she herself had been confined. The old adage of looking a gift horse in the mouth might again well apply. It would be good to no longer have to avoid the girl. "I accept your apology. Thank you for being brave enough to say that."

Cora nodded, suddenly looking a little shy. "Mayhap we could walk a bit and talk?"

Why not? It wasn't overly cold, and she'd dressed for the weather. It would feel good to stretch her legs after the cramped space of a single room. "Yes. Let's."

They walked past the makeshift temporary barracks and across the small field that was used for training and reached the forest line. Cora stopped and tilted her head questioningly.

"Would ye like to see the cottage where the old healer lived? 'Tis nae too far."

"I haven't seen it, but why would I want to?"

Cora shrugged. "We doona have to go there. I just thought, since the woman was accused—*falsely*, ye ken—of witchcraft, it might be good just to see how ordinary her cottage was." She gave another half-shrug. "Just to prove all of this talk about witches to be nonsense."

Thea supposed that made sense in a way. Maybe Cora was the one who needed to see the cottage and realize that the healer had just been an ordinary woman. She needed the walk anyway.

"Lead on, then."

Cora smiled and gestured. "This way."

They'd gone nearly a mile, following a narrow deer trail, when the thatched-roof cottage came into sight. It stood in a small clearing, looking a little lonely and forlorn with its dilapidated paint, closed shutters, and vegetation dead along the front of it. Thea tried to imagine it in the summertime, with a full herb garden and its windows open to let in the sunshine and warm air.

"It was probably very pretty when the woman lived here, but more than likely it's locked up." Thea turned to leave.

"Wait." Cora said. "Let's check. I'd like to see the inside for myself."

Thea hesitated, not liking to enter someone's home without permission, even if it were abandoned. But, if it would help put Cora's final apprehensions to rest, then it might be worth it. She backtracked and followed Cora to the front stoop.

Cora tried the handle and the door swung outward. "See? It's open." She gestured. "After ye."

Thea stepped inside. She'd taken no more than a few steps when the door slammed shut behind her, leaving her in utter darkness. And then she heard Liam's voice from somewhere in the room.

"And now ye will pay, ye little witch. Now ye will pay."

Chapter Twenty

Ian took a satisfied breath and laid the latest missives down on his desk. General Murray had called off the siege on Blair Castle and returned to Inverness to join the prince and Ardsheal. As much as he understood Scots were divided in their support of either the Cause or the government, it was still disheartening to think Murray was firing on his own clan seat. Ian was glad he'd decided to retreat.

Even better news, though, was that Cromartie had taken Dunrobin Castle and caused William Sutherland, the clan chief, to flee. According to that letter, Sutherland had barely managed to escape via the postern gate, taking only what he wore on his back. No doubt he'd try to connect to Cumberland's forces, but at least one stronghold to the north would no longer pose a threat.

Both were good news, and Ian was equally glad that things had settled down at Kilcoy. Cromartie had originally left Ardsheal in charge, but when his cousin went to join the prince's forces, Ian had become the de facto commander. Not exactly a laird, since the earl didn't use that term, but definitely in charge of everything that went on, both at the castle and the surrounding crofters who paid allegiance.

And he'd finally been able to release Thea what she called imprisoned custody. She'd looked incredibly happy this morning as they were breaking their fast, and something strange had fluttered in his chest. His own mood had been dour while he'd kept her confined, partly because he knew she didn't like being stuck inside four walls and also partly because he hadn't been able to convince her she was safer in those four walls. But tensions had de-escalated and his own mood had considerably lightened.

He rose from his chair. Perhaps he'd go find Thea and ask if she wanted to go for a ride. Being cooped up as she had been, she'd probably welcome a gallop in the fresh snow that had fallen overnight. He grinned at the aspect of maybe even having a snowball fight when they returned.

A few minutes later, though, he was frowning. Thea hadn't been in the Great Hall or the smaller dining room. He'd knocked on her door, and when she hadn't answered, he'd opened it to find the room empty. So was the solar. Where was she? Maybe she was with Moire.

He found her in the kitchen, waiting for the cook to take out a pan of fresh scones. "Do ye ken where Thea is?"

Moire gestured toward the door while keeping an eye on the oven. "She said she wanted to go outside and get some fresh air."

"Good." That would mean she'd already be dressed for the weather. "I think I'll join her."

"Mmmm," Moire answered, her mouth full of scone.

When he went to the garden, though, there was no sign of her, although he'd followed a set of boot prints in the snow. At the bench, he saw a second pair of prints. A cloud suddenly passed over the sun, dimming the landscape. He looked up to see the sky darkening. A storm was arising out of nowhere. Thea had no idea how fast a blizzard could form in late spring. Where was she?

And who was with her? The second set of prints was as small as Thea's, which indicated another woman. The only other female, besides the staff, was Cora. Had she come out here too? He hadn't seen her anywhere in the castle. He looked to where both sets led off toward the barracks and set off to follow them. When he got to the field, he saw that both sets had crossed it, heading toward the trees.

Why would they—whoever the second person was—be going into the forest? The hair at his nape began to prickle. He suddenly had a feeling that the storm wasn't the only danger Thea was facing.

He began to run.

****

Thea tested the bonds that had her tied securely to a chair. Although her hands were free, Liam had tied the rope in several tight knots behind her and warned her to keep her hands on the table in front of her. Since she wasn't sure how volatile he might be—so far, he'd been calm—she didn't want to find out. He'd lit an oil lamp and started a small fire in the hearth to heat some water, so obviously he was not in any hurry to leave. Maybe she could reason with him.

"Why are you doing this?" She tried to keep her voice calm and conversational.

"Ye killed my son," he replied in an equally conversational manner.

Somehow, the civil tone made her wary. This was a man who was acting deliberately, not emotionally. Was that good or bad? She watched as he poured hot water into a cup and then picked up a tin can to scoop out some of its contents. Her blood chilled when she recognized it as one of her canisters from the pantry—a canister that Cora must have provided for him. That meant the apology had been a lie to lure Thea here on purpose. Cora had arranged this whole thing.

And then her blood froze when she saw it was hemlock leaves that Liam was stirring into the water.

Liam set the cup down on the table. "I want ye to drink this."

Thea stared at him. "You know drinking that will kill me, right?"

He nodded solemnly. "'Tis only fitting. Ye killed my son with these."

"*No*. No, I didn't. Please listen." Maybe, if she could explain, she could make him understand why Darach had really died. "If you'll let me—"

"Nae." He lifted the cup and moved closer. "'Twould be the honorable thing for ye to drink this yourself—"

"I am not Socrates!"

For a moment, he paused, frowning, then shook his head. "I doona ken who that is, but if ye won't drink it yourself, I will force it down your throat."

"*No*! Wait! Let me—"

"I said *nae*." He moved toward her, one hand grabbing her hair and pulling her head back.

Instinctively, Thea braced against his hand, throwing herself backward and kicked both feet into his groin. The cup went flying as Liam bent over in pain at the same time that the door crashed open.

****

Ian didn't wait for his eyes to adjust to the dim light. He heard the crash of a chair and saw a hulking form bent over. Silently, he dove for the man. It took only an instant to subdue him, thanks to the fact that he was already in pain. Ian flipped him over, placing a knee against his throat and then he widened his eyes.

"Liam? What do ye think ye are doing?"

The man made a gurgling sound, and Ian released some of the pressure. "Answer me before I decide ye willna have more air to breathe!"

"I doona care if ye kill me. Darach and my wife are dead!"

"What?"

"My wife took her life because the witch killed our son!"

"Thea is nae a witch." Before he could say more, two of his men—the blacksmith and the head stablemaster—appeared in the doorway.

"Moire sent us," the blacksmith said as he took in the scene. "What is going on here?"

"I'm trying to find that out myself," Ian said as he stood up. "Watch over him and doona let him move."

As the two men entered to stand guard, Ian went over to Thea and quickly untied her, then helped her up. "Are ye all right?"

"Just a bit bruised," she answered, "but Liam tried to make me drink hemlock. Cora gave him my canister."

"*What*?" He was beginning to sound like a parrot. He turned back to Liam. "Ye had best explain yourself if ye want your life spared."

"Can I sit up? I give ye my word I'll nae try anything."

Ian studied him a moment. "If ye do, ye are dead."

Liam sat up, rubbing his throat. "My wife died two days ago. I was beside myself with grief. Cora came to tell me that the wit…that woman…would be released from her room today. She brought the tin can with her. She said her father was convinced the wit…that woman…practiced witchcraft and the only way to stop her was for her to die."

Ian felt a cold rage building inside him. "Ye planned to kill Thea?"

"It seemed fitting. My son died by hemlock poisoning—"

"No, he did *not*," Thea said. "All the poultice did was stop the bleeding on the outside. Your son was gored by a tusk that tore into his guts. I couldn't tell how deeply, but I suspect he bled to death on the inside."

"'Tis nae what Callum said."

"Callum saw the wound," Thea answered. "He lied to you."

"Well, we will get to the bottom of what Callum said—and what Cora did—when we get back to the castle." Ian tossed the rope that had bound Thea to the two men. "Tie him up and take him to the dungeon. I'll send word to Cromartie, since he's the earl's tenant, and let him decide what to do."

They nodded, the blacksmith hauling Liam up while the stablemaster quickly tied his hands behind him. "We'll make sure he doesna get away."

Ian watched them go, then turned back to Thea and put an arm around her shoulder. He could feel her trembling. "Are ye sure ye are all right?"

"I think so." Her arm curled around his waist and she laid her head against his chest. "Would you just hold me for a moment?"

"Aye, lass." He wrapped both arms around her and laid his head atop hers. "I will hold ye for as long as ye want."

They stood like that for several minutes before she leaned her head back and looked up at him. "Maybe you could build the fire up a bit more?"

For a moment, he wasn't sure which fire she was referring to…the one in the hearth or the one that had started building in his groin ever since he put his arms around her and she'd clung to him. He gave himself a mental shake. She'd just nearly been murdered. She wasn't having wayward thoughts of lust like he was. He raised a brow. "Should we nae be getting back to the castle? 'Twas starting to snow when I arrived."

Thea shook her head. "I don't want to go back yet. I don't really care if we have a blizzard." She looked around the small cottage. "It seems Maggie left the place in good order. The bed looks comfortable." She gave him a quick glance, then looked down and shrugged. "We could spend the night, maybe."

Was she suggesting what he thought she was? He gave himself another mental shake. She probably wasn't. Or maybe…she *was*. It was common for a lot of men to feel lust after a bloody battle. Thea had almost been killed. Maybe she was having the same reaction. Still, he wasn't going to take advantage of that. He brought one of his hands to her shoulder and lifted her chin with his other one, forcing her to look at him.

"Sometimes, after a man nearly loses his life in a fight, he is filled with the need to lay with a woman," he said. "But 'tis a fleeting thing…most just want to assure themselves they are still living. If that is what ye are feeling, I can lie ye down and hold ye for as long as ye want."

"I don't want to just be held." Thea placed a hand

on either side of his face. "I want to feel you inside of me." She leaned up on tiptoe so her mouth was a mere inch from his. "Do you understand?"

He understood. His lips closed over hers, his tongue parting them and plundering her mouth, mimicking the thrusts that he soon would be doing. Like a storm at sea, his desire was building like a dozen rogue waves, threatening to dash the invisible hull that he'd kept around his heart for too long. And he didn't care.

****

Kissing Alan had never been like this. She was feeling a thousand sensations at once, much like plunging into a hot spa tub after nearly freezing on a winter patio. Warmth flooded her veins and she felt as though she were floating on calm water…but maybe that was the softness of the feathers on the bed Ian had just laid her on.

He lost no time in divesting himself of his clothes, although she hardly had time to admire the chiseled planes of his chest and abs, the sculpted muscles of his arms and thighs, or the beauty of his manhood standing at attention: big, thick, and hard as granite. He moved quickly to the bed, removing her clothing almost as quickly as he had his own. There was no need to build the fire in the hearth. Their body heat was practically steaming the air.

For as quickly as she found herself naked, Ian's next movements were slow. He leaned over her, kissing her forehead and then raining kisses over her eyelids and down her cheek before he took her mouth, his lips teasing and nibbling at hers as though he had all the time in the world to savor them. Thea moaned and then grabbed his head, demanding more.

Ian obliged, his tongue sweeping in, deepening the kiss. His hand cupped a breast, kneading softly until it felt heavy and full as a water balloon. She arched her back against the exquisite feeling, and Ian moved his hand to her other breast, fondling it while his thumb flicked across the hardened nipple. She began to whimper as he rolled the first one between his fingers, causing it to bead. His mouth drifted down to nibble a trail along her throat. Thea tilted her head sideways to give him better access and then gasped as his mouth slid lower to take her breast. His tongue laved the pebbled peak, circling before he began to suckle.

If she had been floating in calm seas before, Thea now felt herself practically lifting off the bed, much like a mighty wave raising her to its crest before allowing her down into the trough of satiation before rising even higher as he turned his attention to the other breast. Liquid spread between her thighs, along with a slow, steady vibration.

His mouth moved back to hers as his hand drifted lower, sliding over her hip and across her body. He cupped her mound and rubbed his thumb across her nub, alternating the pressure and pace. And then, her thighs were over his shoulders as he lapped between her legs with slow, long strokes of his tongue. Over and over, like rollers over sandbars, her body pulsed and throbbed, much like the ebb and flow of an undertow, bringing her to the height of sensation before washing her back out to sea.

She trembled, her body beginning to shake uncontrollably, floundering like a rudderless ship, when Ian suddenly sucked her nub deep into his mouth and she shattered.

Thea hardly caught her breath before she felt the tip of his manhood pressing against her soft, open core and he thrust himself fully inside, filling her completely. The thrusts were slow at first, teasing her again, much like waves building in the sea, and then the thrusts became harder and faster as those swells gathered strength and power. Her release hovered on a white-foamed crest before it reached its peak and washed over her before gushing into nothingness as her world went still and she sank to the bottom of her proverbial sea.

Slowly she opened her eyes. "That was *la petite mort*," she whispered. "The little death. It's never happened to me before."

Ian grinned, looking extremely well-pleased with himself. "And it will happen again, I promise."

"Mmmm," she murmured, suddenly sleepy as she curled against his shoulder. "It had better."

****

And it did happen again. Twice more before morning. Ian awoke wondering if perhaps they could have a fourth try. Never in his entire life had he met a woman who so perfectly matched his needs, although at the moment the lass was still soundly asleep and quite probably sore, considering how innovative they'd been.

He glanced at the window, surprised to see the sun streaming in. Perhaps that was what had awakened him. In any case, there was not time for another romp. They needed to return to the castle before Moire sent another contingent out looking for them.

Reluctantly, he roused Thea, who yawned sleepily and reached for him with something that sounded like a very contented purr.

"We've nae time, love," he said, removing her arms

from around his neck, but kissing her palms. "Ye need to get dressed before we have company."

That made her eyes spring open. "Oh, my God. What time is it?"

"Near midmorning, I think."

Thea hopped from the bed and began gathering her clothes. "If I go in the back door, I can get to my bedroom before anyone realizes I wasn't there last night."

Ian put a hand on her arm, stopping her. "'Twill be nae need to hide the fact that we spent the night here. I want to marry ye."

She stared at him, then shook her head. "You are not obligated to marry me because we slept together. In my century, it's quite common to have…relations…without commitment."

"But we are in *my* century and I would honor ye." Ian smiled. "'Tis nae obligation, either. I…" He hesitated, hardly able to believe he really felt the way he did. "I love ye."

"You *love* me?"

He nodded. "I think I have for a long time." He held her gaze. "Will ye marry me?"

Thea was silent for so long that he knew she was going to say no and was probably thinking of a nice way to do it. Then she chewed her lip, making him realize once more how much he desired her. Mentally, he prepared himself for her rejection.

"I didn't think I would ever feel love again," Thea said. "What Alan and I had was special. I realize, though, that my love for him—and probably his for me—was based on having been friends since we were children. We really were more like brother and sister." She smiled suddenly. "It certainly wasn't what I felt last night. I would like a lifetime of that. In *either* century. So, aye, I will marry ye."

He laughed at her attempt of a burr and then picked her up, swung her around, and set her down before kissing her deeply. Then he broke off the kiss before he succumbed to tumbling her again.

"We can continue this once we get back to the castle." He grinned. "Just as soon as we put in an appearance, we can disappear upstairs."

Thea grinned too. "Then we'd better hurry."

However, when they reached the castle, it was in chaos. Mrs. Moffett met them at the door, a worried look on her face. Moire came up behind her.

"'Tis a good thing ye've finally come home," she said as she gave an apprising look at Thea. "Let's talk inside."

With a jolt, Ian remembered he had a prisoner to attend to. When the men brought Liam back last night, no doubt all sorts of rumors arose. Cora needed to be dealt with, as well. His comfortable bedroom upstairs was going to have to wait.

"Ask Callum to join us," he told Mrs. Moffet as they entered the sitting room next to the foyer. When she exchanged looks with Moire, he sensed something was wrong. "What is it?"

"Callum isna here," Moire said.

"Where did he go?"

"We doona ken," Mrs. Moffett answered. "When he didna come to break his fast, I went out to the surgery. It was empty. His things were gone from his room, as well."

Ian frowned. "And Cora?"

"She's gone too," Mrs. Moffett said. "When the

blacksmith brought Liam in last night—he wouldn't tell us why—Cora went white as new snow. Then she said she wasna feeling well and went to bed." She paused. "But I guess she didna."

Ian sighed. "I guess she and her father are miles away from here, then."

"So are ye going to tell what has happened?" Moire asked.

"Aye." He gave her and the housekeeper a grim look. "Cora convinced Liam that Thea killed his son, and she gave Liam hemlock to poison Thea."

Silence followed his statement as they stared at him in shock.

"Why would Cora do that?" Mrs. Moffett finally said.

Moire snorted. "The stupid girl thought Ian would marry her."

"What?" he asked incredulously. "I never encouraged her. I didna ken—"

"Just because ye ignored her doesna mean she took that as an answer."

"But why would she pursue me, then?"

Moire rolled her eyes. "Ye can be quite dense at times, Ian Stuart. Ye and your cousin Ardsheal have rich lands at Appin. 'Twould have been a prestigious match for Cora. But then Thea came and ye were besotted."

"I was nae…" He caught himself and smiled at Thea. "Well, I guess I was. I'll nae deny it now." He turned back to Moire. "We are betrothed."

While Mrs. Moffett gasped, Moire didn't look at all surprised. She just smiled. "I guess ye'll have to decide where to live, then."

And suddenly, another jolt of reality hit Ian. Moire

wasn't referring to a building or property. She was referring to which century it would be.

Chapter Twenty-One

Thea studied Ian's cousin covertly as Ardsheal
seated himself at Ian's desk—actually, she supposed it
was Ardsheal's desk—and wondered if she'd be able to
convince him to persuade the prince not to fight at
Culloden. Or at least not to fight on Drummossie Moor.
History didn't say what the outcome would be if they
chose a different location.

She'd almost forgotten how tall and muscular
Ardsheal was, and he was reputed to be one of the
strongest of Highland warriors, able to brandish a
claymore as though it were no more than a child's
wooden sword. Did that mean he would prefer to charge
forward like an angry bull, or would he be able to listen
to reason? She had coached Ian on what questions to ask,
since women had few rights in this century and certainly
were not asked for their opinions on war strategies. Much
as it pained her, Thea knew better than to try to convince
him herself—her friend Vi would probably have done so
anyway—but stopping the battle that would happen on
April sixteenth was more important than her ego.
Especially since today was the fifteenth.

Ian glanced at her before addressing his cousin.
"With the news that Cromartie was ambushed on his way
here from Dunrobin and is being held hostage, is the
prince sure he wants to march to meet Cumberland on
the morrow? He'll be one general short."

"Murray did bring up that point," Ardsheal said, "but the prince, as ye ken, doesna usually agree with him. And Colonel Sullivan thinks meeting Cumberland when he doesna expect it will be to the prince's advantage."

"What is Murray's advice?" Thea asked even though she already knew.

"He has advised that we doona march head-on but use Robert the Bruce's tactics of lying in wait and then ambush in full Highland charge as Cumberland advances."

"That sounds like a good idea, especially since it worked for Bruce," she replied and gave Ian a prodding look.

"Aye." He added quickly, "'Tis the way Scots have won many battles. The moor gives the advantage to the English, especially their cavalry." He glanced at Thea again. "Our men fight mainly afoot. We'd be at a disadvantage. Mayhap ye could try and get the prince to change his mind?"

"I already tried that. So did Murray." Ardsheal shrugged. "I suppose ye could say we reached a compromise."

"Oh?" Thea practically felt her ears perk. Was it possible that history would be changed?

"Aye. We ken that Cumberland is already at Nairn. But today is the duke's birthday as well, and he will nae doubt be celebrating. 'Tis hardly a dozen miles from camp to Nairn, so the prince has decided we march tonight and surprise Cumberland at dawn before his troops can muster."

No! Thea bit her lip hard to not shout the word. She'd forgotten that attempt would be made and that it failed because the prince would get a late start waiting for more soldiers to arrive and wouldn't make it to Nairn before dawn and would have to retreat. It was the worst thing they could do. Frantically, she looked at Ian. His expression grew puzzled since she hadn't told him about this incident. He turned back to Ardsheal.

"Do ye think it wise to march at night? The duke may have scouts posted along the way since he'll probably march on Inverness tomorrow?"

"The prince is hoping the man will be too inebriated tonight to rouse himself or his men early, and we can catch him by surprise." He pushed back his chair and stood to leave. "'Tis why I came. The prince wants ye to join him."

****

Thea hadn't expected sleep to come, and it hadn't. By dawn the next morning—the *fatal* morning unless, by some miracle, the prince's surprise attack worked—she was up, dressed in men's trews to better maneuver, and had a bag stuffed with as many poultices, bandages, and other medicinal items as she could carry. Even if the Jacobites had been successful—and she'd spent most of the night's waking hours praying they would be—there would still be wounded. Better to meet them on the road than wait for them to come to her.

A stable lad—the adult men had all gone with Ardsheal and Ian yesterday—was too sleepy to question where she might be going before the sun was up. She was grateful for that small favor since she wasn't about to be waylaid by some stupid argument about women riding alone. She'd left a note for Moire so she wouldn't worry, but she'd deliberately not told her of the plan to meet the returning men, because Moire would have wanted to come. Better she, at least, be safe at Kilcoy.

Snow had begun falling and the wind started to pick up as she rode out, but Thea ignored it and started praying again. Even more important than attending the wounded, she needed to find Ian and make sure he was alive. Now that she'd found love once more, she didn't want to lose him too.

As she neared Culloden, she—thankfully—spotted him almost immediately at the edge of the moor. He saw her too and came running.

"What are ye doing here?" he demanded once they'd embraced. "Ye need to go back."

Thea shook her head. "Callum is gone. I'm the closest thing you have for a medic. I will not let someone die if I can help it."

"Nae a one of us is wounded. Ye need to go home."

Instead of answering him, she looked around, dismay and dread filling her at what she saw. It was true that no one was injured, but men were lying on the ground or sitting hunched over against the cold and the few that were standing looked exhausted. She looked at Ian.

"What happened last night?"

He sighed. "The prince was nae satisfied with the numbers and sent for more men. By the time we headed out, Murray kenned we'd nae make it to Nairn before dawn, but the prince wouldna listen. We were at least still two miles away when the sun rose."

She stared at him. "That means all of you marched nearly twenty miles roundtrip last night." She looked around. "These men are tired and, I'm sure, hungry."

"Aye. Some of them are out hunting and some have gone to the nearest village for vittles."

"Why not just have everyone return to camp?" she

asked as an icy pellet hit her cheek. "It's beginning to sleet. Maybe Cumberland will wait another day."

Ian nodded and gestured to where the commanders stood across the moor from them. "'Tis what Murray is trying to persuade the prince to do. Even Sullivan is nae arguing the point."

Thea said another quick prayer. History could be changed if even one of the commanders could just convince the prince to retreat and wait another day...

Her fervor was broken by a rider galloping recklessly across the slippery ground, his horse nearly going down as he managed to rein in. "Cumberland is on the march!" he shouted. "He nears the moor!"

****

All hell suddenly broke loose. Murray, Drummond, Sullivan, and others in command of smaller units scattered, shouting to their men to get into formation. Murray took charge of the right flank, which was usually MacDonald privilege, but they'd moved to the left. Chattans formed the center front line, with Frasers, Farquarsons and Mackintoshs behind them.

Ian saw Ardsheal's unit join Murray. He should be joining them, but he couldn't leave Thea unattended.

"Ye really need to leave. *Now*. Before the battle breaks."

"No."

"I've nae time to argue with ye, Thea. I need to join my cousin."

"Then do so."

Ian shook his head. "I cannae, with ye still here."

"I promise I'll stay well out of harm's way," Thea replied. "But it's imperative I'm close by to help with the wounded."

He looked across the moor again. This time, he caught Ardsheal's eye. His cousin gestured to Thea and then nodded to Ian, signaling that he stay with her.

He nodded back in understanding. Since he'd been training men and not commanding them, he'd merely be another soldier. And someone had to protect Thea.

Cumberland's army appeared on the horizon, a red misty line, through the swirling snow and sleet, that grew larger as they approached. Ian stared at the massive army of foot and the huge number of cavalry behind them. He'd heard Cumberland had at least seven thousand troops. The prince had less than five, and many of those were still foraging for food. Nor did the Scots have a lot of horses. They would have to depend on the charge.

But there was no call to charge. The prince, who was at the edge of the moor, had not issued the order. Did he not understand how Scots fought? And then suddenly there was a shout from the center line as the Chattans ran forward, shields in front of them, swords high. At the same time, some of Murray's men broke loose, but they'd miscalculated.

Ian's eyes widened as the right flank neared the wall of the Leanach enclosure and were forced to veer to the left, colliding with the Chattans' center charge. A melee ensued, with men swarming around each other, trying to reorganize.

And then the English army began to move. Ian watched in horror as the foot soldiers engaged the Scots while the cavalry surrounded them, slowly forming a loop around the battle, and began to squeeze them in, cutting off any chance of escape. Men's screams pierced the air. The sound was deafening.

And then—suddenly—there was silence. Eerily, the

snow thickened so all he could see was white, shutting off the battlefield altogether.

Beside him, Thea clutched his arm. "What is happening? I can't see or hear anything."

"'Tis because the battle is finished," a voice said.

They both whirled at the sound, to see the auburn-haired woman who had helped Thea at the perfumery weeks ago.

"What are ye doing out here?" he asked. "'Tis a war going on."

"'Tis finished," she said again. "Ye can do nothing here. 'Tis time to leave."

"But I have to attend the wounded," Thea protested.

"'Tis too late for that." The woman shook her head sadly. "I have to send ye back to your future."

Thea stared at her. "*You* brought me here? How?"

"I am the goddess Bridgid. I tried, but I couldna stop what happened here. In your time there may still be hope for Scotland to be free." She turned to Ian. "Do ye want to help Niall Fraser and Robbie Mackintosh free Scotland?"

Ian furrowed his brows. "Aye. But how?"

She studied him. "They await ye in Thea's time—"

"In my time?" Thea interrupted. "How did they get there?'

The goddess smiled. "They are soul mates of your friends, Charlotte Campbell and Vihansa Sutherland."

Thea stared at her. "My friends are here?"

"Nae more. I sent them back. 'Tis now your turn." She turned to Ian. "Do ye want to go with Athena to the future?"

"Aye," he replied with no hesitation and put his arm around Thea. "I want to be with my love, regardless of who or what awaits us."

Bridgid smiled and lifted her arms high. "*Gum faigh thu sith, taibhse cuil lodair.*"

She smiled as the mist enveloped them completely. "May ye find peace, Ghost of Culloden."

Epilogue

Thea watched Ian and his friends standing out on the patio of her Dallas townhouse, experimenting with the taste of modern ale, and then turned to Charlotte and Vi.

"It's hard to believe that we were all there…in their time."

"Unbelievable," Charlotte agreed. "I'm going to write a novel about it."

"Fiction, I hope," Thea replied. "I doubt anyone would believe it was nonfiction."

"Duh. We'd probably be carted off to the nearest mental ward." Charlotte grinned suddenly. "That's why the romance genre is so great. Anything can happen."

"Unfortunately, we couldn't make happen what Bridgid hoped we could," Vi said. "As grateful as I am that I was able to actually experience history—and meet Robbie, of course—I wish we could have made a difference at Culloden."

Charlotte sobered. "I wish we could have too, but even with a goddess on our side—a *real* goddess from the ancient Celts—it still didn't help." She sighed. "I guess history wasn't meant to be changed."

"Perhaps not," Thea said, "but that doesn't mean we can't shape the future." Her friends looked at her, Charlotte with a curious expression and Vi more speculatively. "I mean, think of it. Ian is a Stuart… he was a direct relative of Bonnie Prince Charlie in the eighteenth century. With all the DNA technology available, he can be tested. If his results show a close connection, he could claim he's the heir to the Scottish crown."

"Except that Scotland happens to be a part of the United Kingdom," Charlotte reminded her.

"Actually, the Stuarts didn't concede their right to succession with the Acts of Union of 1707," Vi said, "and they never have given up their right to a Scottish crown."

Thea nodded speculatively. "And, there are still those who think Scotland should be independent. If Ian's DNA provides a direct link, he could petition the British government. Niall and Robbie could circulate words among the Frasers, Farquarsons, and Mackintoshes for support."

Vi raised an eyebrow. "You want an uprising?"

Thea shook her head and fingered the Greek key necklace she'd dug out of her jewelry box when she and Ian had returned to this century. The design of horizontal and vertical lines that were always connected and never ending was symbolic of infinity. A Greek saleslady had also told her it meant that life had its ups and downs. Scotland had certainly had those. And if the Stuart line was unbroken, couldn't that be viewed as infinite? "No violence. Maybe a peaceful transfer of a legitimate right, though? There would be proof of legitimacy with the DNA—"

"That's a really long shot," Vi said.

"But what if it could happen?" Charlotte asked. "Just think! Another Stuart on the Scottish throne!"

"A Highlander unconquered," Thea added. "*My* Highlander."

Vi snorted. "You daydream too much. Both of you. It'll never happen."

"No?" Charlotte raised a brow. "*Stranger* things have happened, and just recently." She gestured to the Ian, Niall, and Robbie standing outside.

Vi pursed her mouth. "I suppose you do have a point."

"But what if it *could*? What if Ian could prove he was a direct—albeit three centuries apart—descendent? And our children would inherit, as well." Thea said. "Scotland would have achieved what it couldn't at Culloden."

Charlotte nodded. "Maybe that's why Bridgid sent us back. The timing wasn't right in Bonnie Prince Charlie's time. Maybe it is now."

Vi looked at both of them thoughtfully, finally giving them a wry smile. "You may be right. It's worth a try." She picked up her glass to offer a toast. "To the future then. Scotland. Forever."

Charlotte and Thea raised theirs too.

"Scotland. Forever."

Afterword

Charles Stuart V of Ardsheal was attainted for high treason on 8 June, 1746, and spent several weeks hiding in a cave on his estate before fleeing to France where his wife and children were eventually able to join him. The English sacked and burned his castle, destroying almost all records of his accomplishments. He died in exile in 1757.

After Culloden, Bonnie Prince Charlie escaped to the Isle of Skye, then to France, and finally to Italy where he used the alias of Count of Albany—a reference to his lineage from Mary, Queen of Scots, and her second husband, Henry Stuart, Lord Darnley, Duke of Albany. Although the prince was legitimately married to Princess Louise of Stolberg-Gedern, his only heir was Charlotte, the illegitimate daughter of his mistress, Clementina. He eventually recognized his daughter, styling her the Duchess of Albany. Charlotte, in turn, had three illegitimate children with Ferdinand Maximillian de Rohan, Archbishop of Cambrai.

It is through this connection that a man living in Belgium claimed to be a direct descendant of Bonnie Prince Charlie. His claim has been debunked.

In 1913, the Stuart dynasty did relinquish the right to the English crown, but *not* to Scotland's.

Bonnie Prince Charlie was known to have had several mistresses, so perhaps a descendant does exist somewhere…

Scotland. Forever.

Thank you for purchasing
this publication of The Wild Rose Press, Inc.

For questions or more information
contact us at
info@thewildrosepress.com.

The Wild Rose Press, Inc.